SCREECH OWLS

# MYSTERY AT LAKE PLACID

## ROY MacGREGOR

Tundra Books

First published by McClelland & Stewart, 1995
Published in this edition by Tundra Books, 2013

Text copyright © 2013 by Roy MacGregor

Published in Canada by Tundra Books, a division of Random House of Canada Limited,
a Penguin Random House Company

Published in the United States by Tundra Books of Northern New York, a division of
Random House of Canada Limited, a Penguin Random House Company

Library of Congress Control Number: 2012943703

**Library and Archives Canada Cataloguing in Publication**

MacGregor, Roy, 1948-
        Mystery at Lake Placid / Roy MacGregor.

(Screech Owls)
ISBN 978-1-77049-413-8

        I. Title. II. Series: MacGregor, Roy, 1948- Screech Owls series.

PS8575.G84M98 2013        jC813'.54        C2012-904864-X

We acknowledge the financial support of the Government of Canada through the
Canada Book Fund and that of the Government of Ontario through the Ontario
Media Development Corporation's Ontario Book Initiative. We further acknowledge
the support of the Canada Council for the Arts and the Ontario Arts Council for
our publishing program.

ONTARIO ARTS COUNCIL
CONSEIL DES ARTS DE L'ONTARIO

Designed by Jennifer Lum

www.penguinrandomhouse.ca

Printed and bound in the United States of America

2 3 4 5 6        18 17 16 15

For Ellen, Kerry, Christine, Jocelyn, Gordon –
and for all the minor-league hockey teams that
have put up with me over the years.


The author is grateful to Doug Gibson for the
notion of this series, and to Lynn Schellenberg,
for her guidance and fine editing,
and to Peter Buck, for his copyediting.

The source of the Klingon words used by
Larry Ulmar is *The Klingon Dictionary* by
Marc Okrand, Pocket Books (New York, 1985).

# 1

"Wedgie stop!"

Travis Lindsay could not believe his ears.

"WEDDD-GEEE stop!"

The big Ford van had been traveling non-stop since the last bathroom break – and Travis had no idea how long ago that had been. He knew only that they had finally turned off that boring four-lane highway and that, far in the distance over the trees, the high green bridge over the St. Lawrence River was now visible.

Beyond lay New York State and the road to Lake Placid. Finally.

Travis had fallen asleep as they drove. He'd had the craziest series of dreams, the kind you always have when half asleep and half awake, head bobbing and eyes drifting. He had dreamed he'd finally found his father's long-lost hockey card collection, the one he searched high and low for, without success, every visit to his grandmother's old house in the country. He had dreamed he was back in grade six, that he had failed his year, and that he was failing again because someone had stolen all his workbooks from his locker. And he had dreamed he was taking a face-off in the Olympic Center in Lake Placid – the American Stars and Stripes and the Canadian Maple Leaf flying high overhead, the two anthems still echoing in the rafters, in the stands his mother and father, his teachers, his friends from school, NHL scouts, Wayne Gretzky and Bobby Orr and Gordie Howe, Alex Ovechkin and Sidney Crosby, Claude Giroux, the *Hockey Night in Canada* crew – and just as the referee held out the puck, Travis looked down at the circle and saw that *he had forgotten to put on his skates!*

His toes were blue! His feet were wiggling and slipping on the cold ice surface. But no one else had noticed! The referee's skates dug in, sending ice chips flying. The other center's skates kicked in toward the circle, the skate heading toward Travis's toes with more sharp blades than a Swiss Army knife.

NNNNOOOOOOO! . . .

Travis had woken up in the van shouting, and everyone on the Screech Owls had laughed and slapped at his shoulders and the back of his head. He had refused to tell them what had scared him. Let them think whatever they wanted. It was a ridiculous dream anyway. He'd never forget his skates. Besides, he wasn't even a center.

Mr. Dillinger had been driving since they left Tamarack and would be driving until they got there. He would have to – Mr. Dillinger was the only one in the rented twelve-seater van old enough to have a license. Muck and the assistant coaches, the other parents who were coming, and four of the players were in other cars, some far ahead, some somewhere behind. Travis was secretly pleased that his mother and father had decided not to come, because now he got to travel with the team for once – and delighted, too, that Mr. Dillinger was in charge of the rented van.

Travis looked ahead three seats to where Mr. Dillinger was sitting. He certainly didn't look like a kid – what kid has curly gray hair, a bald spot, and a potbelly big as a hockey bag? – but he sure did act like one. He had started the trip with a "Stupid Stop," pulling off and parking by a little variety store and then standing by its entrance handing out coins and small bills with only one instruction: "Remember, it's a 'Stupid Stop.' I want you to spend every cent of it in one place on something cheap and useless that won't last."

Travis had bought a gummy hand that he could flip ahead two seats, past Derek Dillinger, who was reading quietly, and wrap right around the face of his best friend, Wayne Nishikawa. "Nish," the sickest mind by far on the Screech

Owls, had bought a pen with a bathing beauty on it and when you turned the pen upside-down the bathing suit seemed to peel off. But you couldn't see anything.

Mr. Dillinger had old music like "Weird Al" Yankovic singing silly songs like "Jurassic Park" and "Bedrock Anthem" and "Young, Dumb & Ugly." He had licorice, red and black, to hand back, cold pop in the cooler, and comic books – *X-Men, Batman, Superman,* even a *Mad* magazine – for them to read. He had pillows packed for anyone who, like Travis, wanted to snooze, and, best of all, he had the most outrageous sense of humor Travis or any of the other kids had ever seen in an adult. Not once had anyone whined, "Are we there yet?"

Mr. Dillinger made the perfect team manager. He even made the best jokes himself about his lack of hair, one time showing up for a tournament with a T-shirt that said, "THAT'S NO BALD SPOT – IT'S A SOLAR PANEL FOR A SEX MACHINE." He was fun and funny, but serious when it mattered. Because he also served as the team trainer,

Mr. Dillinger knew first aid. Nish's parents believed he had probably saved Nish from being crippled the year before when he crashed head-first into the boards and Mr. Dillinger refused to let the game continue until an ambulance came. They had carried Nish off the ice on a stretcher, treating him like a cracked egg about to spill. Then their ice time ran out and the game had to be called with the score still tied. Some of the other parents – mostly from the other team, but also loud Mr. Brown, Matt's father – had been yelling for them to get Nish off the ice so the game could continue. The two young referees had looked like they were going to cave in, but Mr. Dillinger had angrily ordered them to clear the ice of players so that no one could slip and fall onto Nish. It turned out that Nish had a hairline fracture of his third vertebrae – almost a broken neck – but thanks to Mr. Dillinger taking charge he hadn't needed anything more than a neck brace and a couple of months off skates and Nish was right back, better than ever. Nish adored Mr. Dillinger.

Mr. Dillinger organized the car pools, made the telephone calls, printed up the schedules and handed them out and replaced those ones the players lost. He ran the fund-raisers – if Travis never saw another bottle drive he'd be happy – and he taped the sticks and sharpened the skates. He sewed the names on the sweaters, washed the sweaters, and even got a local computer company to sponsor the Screech Owls. The computer company had bought the team jackets and hats and redesigned the logo so it looked, Travis and the rest of the team thought, better than most of the NHL crests and almost as good as – Travis thought just as good as – the San Jose Sharks' and the Anaheim Ducks'.

"Wedgie stop!"

"WEDDD-GEEE stop!"

Mr. Dillinger was still shouting and laughing as he put the big van in park and hopped out onto the shoulder of the road. He ran around to the front of the van, bending over and wiggling so his big belly rippled right through his shirt, and with his hands pulling at the seat of his pants, he pretended to be yanking a huge "wedgie" of bunched-up underwear out of his rear end.

Howling with laughter, the team followed suit, a dozen young players out on the side of the road yanking at their pants to free up their underwear and wiggling their rear ends at the other cars that roared by, the drivers and passengers either staring out as if the Screech Owls should be arrested or else pretending the Screech Owls were not even there, a dozen youngsters at the side of the road, bent over, with a hand on each side of their pants, pulling wedgies.

"All 'board!" Mr. Dillinger hollered as he jumped in the van. The team scrambled back in, Nish and several others laughing so hard they had tears in their eyes.

Mr. Dillinger started up the van, then turned, his face unsmiling, voice as serious as a vice-principal's.

"The United States of America takes wedgies very seriously," he announced. "At the border they will ask you where you were born and whether or not you are having any difficulty with your underwear. If they suspect you are having problems, you will be body searched. If they find any wedgies, you will spend the rest of your life . . ."

He paused, waiting.

Nish finished for him: ". . . in prison?"

Mr. Dillinger stared, then smiled: "In Pampers, Nish, in Pampers."

# 2

There had been no "wedgie check" at the American border. A guard had come out and looked in all the windows and guessed, accurately, that they were on their way to Lake Placid for a hockey tournament. He had asked where they were from and where they were born and Mr. Dillinger, organized as always, had passed over a clipboard with a photocopy of everyone's birth certificate.

Mr. Dillinger even had the passports of Fahd

Noorizadeh and Dmitri Yakushev, who weren't yet full Canadian citizens. Fahd boasted he would be the first Saudi Arabian to make the NHL. Dmitri said he would be around the five-hundredth Russian and liked to joke that by the time he got there Canadians would be the exceptions in the NHL and people would be complaining that they were taking jobs from Russian boys.

Dmitri had a weird sense of humor. He was a thin, blond kid with a crooked smile and, Travis figured, the fastest skater in the league. He had started to play hockey back in Moscow and came to Canada at age nine with his parents, so he couldn't really claim to be a product of either system, the Russian or the Canadian. His uncle had once played for the Soviet Red Army team and Dmitri planned to be one of the best hockey players in the world, like him. Right now he was just one of the best hockey players in Tamarack.

But the Screech Owls were a pretty good team. Once, in the back of his Language Arts notebook on an afternoon when the class was supposed to be reading ahead, Travis had even done a scouting report on them:

## GOAL

*Guy Boucher:* Quick hands, great blocker. Yells a lot while playing. Two different ways of saying both names. "Guy," or "Gee," like in Lafleur, and "Bowcher" or "Boo-shay," depending on where he's playing. No one ever knows how his name's going to come out over the public address.

*Sareen Goupa:* Back-up. Good stick and pads, but misses high shots and can be deked pretty easily. Still, pretty good for having played only two years. Team sometimes calls her "Manon" after Manon Rhéaume, the first woman goaltender to play an NHL exhibition game.

## DEFENSE

*Wayne Nishikawa:* "Nish" is the steadiest of all the Screech Owls. Not a really fast skater, but a good shot and very good in front of his own net. Clean player, dirty mind.

*Larry Ulmar:* Nish's usual partner. Slow but a good passer. Lets other team go too much. Nickname is "Data." Obsessed with the classic *Star Trek* series. Claims he can speak Klingon and sometimes tries. Sometimes plays like a Klingon, too.

*Norbert Philpott:* The team's "Captain Video" – Norbert's father owns a video rental outlet and sometimes shoots the games and they show the videos during team get-togethers. Norbert has to analyze everything. As for his own play, he's not very flashy, but he works hard and everyone on the team likes him.

*Willie Granger:* The team's trivia expert. Has probably ten thousand hockey cards in his collection and also has a lot of autographs – from Jean Béliveau to Steven Stamkos and Taylor Hall – which his uncle, a sportswriter in Toronto, gets for him. Willie is a smart player, if not particularly fast.

If he had a good shot, he'd be on the power play.

*Wilson Kelly:* Tremendous checker. Still learning the game, but improving all the time. Always in position. Plans on becoming the first Jamaican to compete in hockey in the Winter Olympics. But for Canada, he says, not Jamaica.

*Zak Adelman:* Quick, but not a physical presence like Wilson. Wilson can cover when Zak pinches up into the play. Quiet but funny – one of those senses of humor where you usually have to run it through your brain a second time before you realize what he's said.

**FORWARDS**

*Sarah Cuthbertson:* Center and the team's best player. Mother skated for Canada in the 1998 Winter Olympics – speed skating – and she now teaches power skating. Sarah is determined to play for Canada in a future Winter Olympics, now that women's hockey is an official medal sport. She's already been asked to play tournaments for a top Canadian women's hockey team. Best skater on the team. Great playmaker. Pretty good shot, but doesn't use it enough. Team captain.

*Dmitri Yakushev:* First-line right wing. So fast he sometimes runs right over the puck. If Sarah hits him with a breakaway pass, Dmitri is gone. No one ever catches him and hardly anyone ever stops him. Great with his feet, which he says comes from playing soccer instead of summer hockey. Idolizes Alex Ovechkin.

*Travis Lindsay:* Left wing, first line. Good skater, good stickhandler, fair shot. Assistant captain.

*Derek Dillinger:* Second-line center. Good playmaker with a very good shot. Would have more points if on first line and will probably move up once Sarah moves on to play for a top women's team. Because of strength, is the face-off man used in tight situations. Hooked on video games. Quieter and more serious than his father.

*Matt Brown:* Left wing. Great shot. Lacks speed. Doesn't like to carry the puck, but get it to him and it's in. Muck has benched him in the past for lazy back-checking.

*Fahd Noorizadeh:* Third-line right wing, first-line computer expert. Produces printouts of everything from goals and assists to plus-minus and chances. Muck thinks this is ridiculous: "The only numbers that matter," Muck says, "are the two they flash up on the scoreboard." Didn't start playing until nine years old and improving all the time. Great knack for reading play.

*Gordie Griffith:* Third-line center. Big and gawky. Gets noticed because of size. Most penalized player on team, the one the other parents yell at – but he isn't dirty at all. Has some shifty moves and can lift puck over net from the blue line.

*Jesse Highboy:* Right wing. The Screech Owls' newest player, moving into town around Christmas from way up north in James Bay. His dad's a lawyer and

Jesse says he's going to be one, too, and still be in the NHL as the league's first *playing* commissioner. A great team player, cheers everybody. Needs more ice time.

*Mario Terziano:* "The Garbage Collector." Nothing fancy, hardly even noticeable – until there's a big scramble in front of the net and the puck is suddenly loose in the slot. Always has his stick down, always ready. A good-hearted guy who laughs even at himself.

The Screech Owls were even slightly famous, having been written up in the *Toronto Star* during a tournament they'd played in Mississauga. Someone must have called the paper in, because a writer and photographer arrived and talked to all the players, and the next day they were on the front page.

The story in the paper was all about how the Screech Owls represented virtually every part of the country. They had a French-Canadian goaltender. They had different religions. They had players who had come from, or whose parents or grandparents had come from, Japan, Saudi Arabia, Russia, Lebanon, Jamaica, Italy, Great Britain, and Germany. And now this year Jesse Highboy, a Cree, had joined. And they had two girls on the team – three before Jessica Crozier had moved out to Calgary.

The story had seemed ridiculous to Travis – after all, they hadn't even made it as far as the tournament final. And the writer of the article kept referring to them as "Team United Nations," only once using their proper name, the Screech Owls. He had also described Sarah as "too pretty to be taken for a hockey player with her soft eyes and long, tumbling brown hair." But Sarah had got the writer back. The reporter had asked Sarah if it bothered her that women made up more than 50 percent of the population but less than 10 per cent of the Screech Owls.

"Why would it?" Sarah answered. "I've been in on more than 50 percent of the goals."

Travis began dozing off again as the big van headed up into the mountains. He heard Willie Granger, team expert on everything, spouting off facts from the *Guinness World Records* on how the Adirondacks didn't even compare to the really high mountains like the Rockies and Mount Everest. He heard Nish, the team pervert, giggling that two of the rounded hills off in the distance looked like "boobs." Nothing unusual there. Nish was so crazy he once said the face-off circles reminded him of two big boobs out in front of the net.

Travis placed his head against the humming window and asked himself the question he'd been asking since the first year he'd signed up for hockey: when was he ever going to start growing? He had always been small, but he hadn't started worrying about it until he turned peewee. He was twelve going on thirteen. Another school year and he would be headed into high school and – already notably small in the schoolyard of Lord Stanley Public School – he was petrified he wouldn't grow before he got there.

Growing was only one of two serious matters that deeply bothered Travis. The second was his fear of the dark – how many twelve-year-olds still needed a night-light? – but most of the time his fear of the dark was something he could keep to himself and his family. But how could you hide your size?

"Hang in there," his father kept telling him. "You'll grow. I was a late grower. My brothers were late growers. You'll go to sleep one night and wake up the next morning having ripped right out of your clothes."

Travis knew what an exaggeration that was. He knew that his father meant he'd have a late growth spurt that might come over one summer, not a single night, and he knew better than to think he would ever fall asleep a peewee and wake up a bantam in a pair of torn pajamas. But he couldn't help wishing anyway. Wouldn't it be nice if, when they got to Lake Placid, Travis stepped out of the van and his pant cuffs were up around his knees . . .

"PIT STOP!"

Travis jumped. He had been dozing again. His head felt thick, his eyes out of focus. He rubbed them as Mr. Dillinger called again from the driver's seat of the big van.

"Pit Stop! Last one before Lake Placid! Ten minutes! You go now or you go later in your pants – this means you, Nish!"

Travis could hear them giggling. His vision cleared and he saw that everyone in the van was looking back at him. Because he had fallen asleep, obviously. Well, so what? But they wouldn't stop laughing.

"What's so funny?" Travis asked Nish, who had turned around, his face looking like it was about to split.

"Mr. Dillinger. Didn't you hear him?"

It didn't make sense, but Travis let it go. He headed into the restaurant, pushed the door open, saw that everyone in there was laughing at the team coming in – what was the matter with them, never see hockey players in a van? – and decided that he'd better go to the washroom first.

Funny, there was no lineup. Nish and some of the other kids were hanging around outside the door but they didn't seem to want to go in. More like they were waiting. Travis pushed past them through the door, turned to the mirror – and saw immediately what his teammates, and all the people in the restaurant, had been giggling at:

HIS HEAD WAS COVERED IN CREAM!

It had been put on like a cone. Swirled like he was about to be dipped into chocolate at Dairy Queen. He looked like a fool. But it was so light he hadn't felt it. That's why they'd been laughing at him. It was hilariously obvious to everyone but Travis himself, who couldn't even feel it up there.

Travis grabbed a handful of the cream and threw it off his head into the sink. He reached for some paper towels and began rubbing it off.

On the other side of the door, he could hear

the entire team howling with laughter as they imagined his reaction.

Travis smelled his hands. Shaving cream. There was only one person in the Screech Owls van old enough to shave.

Mr. Dillinger.

# 3

Travis was still blotting shaving cream from his hair as the pines gave way and the van began climbing up through a twisting string of motels and motor inns, past a Burger King and McDonald's, up and over a hill and down onto the main street of Lake Placid. They were finally here. The six-hour drive was forgotten. The shaving cream was forgotten. Travis was as wide awake and alert as he would be if the team was just waiting for the Zamboni to finish flooding the ice so the game could begin.

Lake Placid was alive with cars and campers and people. It was still early spring yet it felt like an Ontario tourist town at the height of the season. Traffic barely moved. Shoppers wove through the cars as if the street were a parking lot and the stoplights meaningless. It felt like summer to Travis, after a winter of heavy boots and thick jackets and shoveling snow.

There was a banner stretched high across the street. "WELCOME TO LAKE PLACID'S SIXTH ANNUAL INTERNATIONAL PEEWEE HOCKEY CHAMPIONSHIP." "International" – the word made it seem impossible, more like one of his dreams than reality.

Travis had been playing hockey for six seasons – tyke, novice, atom, and now peewee – and he had got much better each year, if not much bigger. In tyke, with his dad the coach, Travis had started the season holding on to the back of a stacking chair so he wouldn't fall, and he had finished the season the best skater on the team after Sarah Cuthbertson, who had, they all joked, an unfair advantage in her mother.

He knew why: he was the one kid who skated everyday – or at least every chance he got – in the open-air rink behind the school. And when he wasn't on the rink, he was in his basement, stick-handling tennis balls across the concrete and firing pucks against a big plywood board his father had bought and attached to the wall.

Travis Lindsay was hockey-crazy. His favorite team was the Detroit Red Wings. He had all the cards from the years of Steve Yzerman and Sergei Fedorov, but the Detroit team of his dreams played back in the 1950s, more than half a century before he was even born, when "Terrible Ted" Lindsay and "Mr. Hockey," Gordie Howe, were the superstars.

Travis's grandfather had once told him that Ted Lindsay was a distant cousin, which made him an even more distant cousin of Travis's – but a cousin all the same. The same name, the same skills . . . the same size. Ted Lindsay had not been big, either, but he had ended up being known as "Terrible Ted" and was in the Hockey Hall of Fame. "Terrible Travis" didn't sound quite as good, but it was the way Travis secretly liked to think of himself.

He had been through house league. He had played on the atom competitive team for a jerk named Mr. Spratt who called them by their last names and insisted on being called "Coach." He wore a suit while he worked the bench in tournaments – even chewed ice like an NHL coach. He used to scream at the kids until they cried. With his parents' blessing, Travis had quit and gone back to house league.

And then he had tried competitive again. With Muck.

Muck Munro was so unlike "Coach" Spratt that it hardly seemed they played the same game. Muck didn't yell. He laughed at the first player who called him "Coach." He didn't wear suits during games, didn't wear matching track outfits for practices.

According to Guy Boucher's dad, Muck had been a pretty fine junior player at one time, but he had so severely broken his leg in a game that he had had to quit hockey altogether. He still walked with a slight limp.

But Travis could see the ability whenever Muck came out onto the ice with them. He had to favor his bad leg a bit, but Travis had never heard a sweeter sound in his life than when Muck went out onto the still-wet ice and took a few long strides down the rink and into the turn, his skates sizzling like bacon in a frying pan as they dug in and flicked out into the next stride.

Travis had tried to listen to his own skating, but all he could hear was the chop when his blades hit. Nothing smooth, nothing sizzling. He figured he had neither the stride nor the weight. He was too small to sound like Muck.

Muck put the team together. He was the one who got Barry Yonson and Ty Barrett to come on as assistants. Barry had played junior *B* the year before, quitting to concentrate on his school work, but Muck figured, correctly, that Barry missed his ice time and invited him out to help with the team. Barry was great: a big, curly-haired guy with a constant gap-toothed smile and the ability to slap a puck – in the air! – all the way from his own blue line over the net and against the glass at the far end.

Ty Barrett was a bit older but had also once played for Muck. He worked as an assistant manager at the Tim Hortons donut shop and every time they had an early practice he would bring in a box of still-warm Timbits he had picked up on the way to the rink. Though heavy-set and a weak skater, Ty was great at organizing drills. He made them fun, always with the two sides competing against each other for first grabs at the Timbits.

It had been Muck who got Mr. Dillinger to be the team manager and trainer, and that had worked out wonderfully, as well. Mr. Dillinger kept the dressing room loose. He drove the van to the tournaments. He organized the pizza, the pop, the wedgie stops. Travis had never had so much fun playing on a team in his life.

"This is it!" Mr. Dillinger shouted as the van groaned up one more hill and swept into the parking lot of the Holiday Inn. It was a Holiday Inn with a putting green out front, nature trails, a big indoor pool, a Jacuzzi hot tub, an arcade, and, straight back down the hill, the Olympic Center hockey rink. The teams could practically roll out of bed into their dressing rooms.

"Awwwww-righhhhtttt!" all twelve Screech Owls shouted. Nish pumped a fat fist out the side window.

They piled out of the van and into the hotel. Muck was already there, waiting, with his usual Diet Coke in his right hand. Spread out before him on a small table were a dozen or so white envelopes with names and numbers on them.

"Good drive?" Muck asked.

"One close shave," Mr. Dillinger answered. "Right, Travis?"

Mr. Dillinger laughed so hard two women checking in turned to stare, but he didn't care. Travis turned red.

"Check the envelopes," Muck said to the new arrivals. "You'll find your roomies and two keys per room. Soon as you find your rooms you can go on up."

Travis was in with Nish, Wilson, and Data. He couldn't have picked better roommates if the choosing had been left to him.

"One more thing," Muck announced as the players scrambled for their keys. "Don't even try to watch the adult movies on your TVs. We've had the front desk disengage the pay channels for the whole tournament. Understand, Nish?"

Nish kept them up until midnight trying, unsuccessfully, to rewire the television so he could watch the forbidden movies. It had taken Travis a long time to fall asleep. He was just too excited about the tournament. It wasn't his fear of the dark – he'd solved that by going last to the bathroom and then "forgetting" to turn off the light, leaving the door open barely a crack. None of the other boys had complained.

By 6:30 a.m. he was wide awake again. Wide awake and anxious. He checked to see if anyone else was awake. Nish was rolled in his sheets like a tortilla, the only fragment of flesh exposed a single big toe sticking free at the bottom. Wilson, on the other hand, had nothing over him, since Nish had yanked all the blankets to his side during the night, and was rolled up in a ball like a baby. Data was snoring slightly, breathing like an old Klingon.

Travis went into the washroom and wet three washcloths with water as cold as it would run. He squeezed them out and then brought them back into the bedroom where he dropped one on each face and, in the case of Nish, over his big toe.

"Whaaaaa?" called Wilson, who bolted straight up.

"*Jach!*" shouted Data. He even dreamed in Klingon!

Nish didn't stir.

"C'mon, guys," Travis said to the others. "We got an eight o'clock practice."

"I don't have to practice any more," Wilson argued. "I can't get any better."

"Come on, Wils – you want to play in the Olympics, you better find out how slow you are on an Olympic ice surface."

Growling, Wilson threw his pillow at Travis and rolled out of bed. Data was already up and

moving. Wilson and Travis jumped simultane-
ously onto Nish, squashing the Tortilla.

"Hey!" Nish shouted, trapped by his blankets.
"Bug off!"

Nish began to twist violently, going nowhere.
Wils sat on his head, lifted his arm and, with his
open hand cupped under his armpit, made a loud
farting noise that caused Nish to twist and scream
until he bounced right off the bed onto the floor.

With Nish furiously staring up, Wils once
again let one rip from his armpit, with everyone
laughing at poor Nish, who'd taken the sound for
something else.

"Jerk," said Nish.

"Let's go," Travis said.

# 4

Travis Lindsay loved dressing rooms. The smells, the sounds, the anticipation before a game and the satisfaction after: ever since he began playing, Travis had loved that first feeling that came over him as he walked into a hockey dressing room.

He loved the familiarity. He loved to know he had his place and his teammates would expect him to be in it. He loved the insults, the practical jokes, the wicked, Coke-forced belches, the stupid, meaningless, harmless bragging.

Sometimes the feeling was better before a game, when everyone would be coming in at different times – Nish usually first, delivered by his parents, who knew his habits best, and then dawdling until he was the last one dressed. Matt Brown always late, his bigmouthed father in a panic and sharp with Matt as he pushed him to hurry. Fahd sometimes playing games on his tablet until Mr. Dillinger announced the Zamboni was out on the ice, then dressing with all the precision and efficiency of a human computer. Sarah Cuthbertson arriving fully dressed but for her shoulder pads, sweater, gloves, helmet, and skates. Willie Granger with some obscure fact he'd memorized from the *Guinness World Records,* like the world's longest sneezing fit being 978 days or something. Travis particularly liked it when everyone would finish dressing in near silence, everyone knowing that there was nothing now but a few words from the coach and a game to come.

Sometimes he liked it best after a game – after a victory, anyway – when he could take as much time as he wanted, sitting there grinning and sweaty, his hands in his lap, his helmet, sweater, shoulder pads, elbow pads, and gloves all off, everything else including his skates still on and tied up tight. Travis loved the feeling of a game well played, the way they would all go over the best plays and the goals and about how well Guy or Sareen had played in goal.

Players would explain missed opportunities ("I couldn't get the puck to lie down," "That ice was terrible, the puck skipped right over my stick") and they would talk about players on the other side ("Did you see his face when he got that penalty?") and hope, always, that maybe someone would say something good about the way they had played. And usually someone did. The Screech Owls were, after all, a team.

Travis had a thing about arenas. He loved the warmth and the light when the door opened for a 6:00 a.m. practice in the winter. He loved the cool and the dark when the door opened for a 6:00 p.m. practice in the early fall. He loved the smell of Dustbane when the workers were cleaning up. He loved the sound a wide broom made when it was pushed across a smooth cement floor. He loved the dry, sparking smell of the sharpening stone when it hit against a skate blade, especially if Mr. Dillinger was doing the sharpening, and he loved to watch how silently, smoothly Mr. Dillinger could work the skate holder across the shiny steel surface of the sharpener.

But more than anything else, Travis loved new ice. He liked to stand with his face against the glass while the Zamboni made its final circle. He liked to watch while the water glistened under the lights and then froze. He loved to be first onto the ice and feel the joy of new ice as he went into his first corner, coming out of it with a fine turn so he could then skate backwards to center, watching the first marks form on the fresh surface – *his* marks.

He liked the first feel of a puck on his stick. He did not like, but could do nothing about, pucks sticking in water that had yet to freeze. Sometimes a player would be about to take a slap shot when the puck would suddenly grip on him, and player and stick would go gliding on alone, the stick swinging down on air. When other players saw that happening, they always roared with laughter. It was embarrassing, but it happened to everyone.

Travis already had superstitions. He was still a long way from legendary Montreal Canadiens' goaltender Patrick Roy talking to his posts, but Travis had a few things he always had to do. This year he had to ring a shot off the crossbar. If he could do that in practice or in the warm-up, then he'd have a good game.

Travis had never seen a rink like this one before. Massive, white, more like an art gallery than a hockey arena. They'd walked by the hall of fame. They'd stood by the Olympic display watching the video repeat the 4–3 win over the Soviet Union that had given the Americans the 1980 Olympic gold medal. None of the Screech Owls had ever seen such a celebration – not when they won, not even when they watched the Stanley Cup playoffs and saw the Rangers or the Penguins or the Canadiens win.

The win had been called "The Miracle on Ice." And it looked like a miracle. The place had filled with thousands of blue and white balloons. The crowd had poured onto the ice. The players were in tears. Men and women – who were they? fathers? mothers? officials? – crying and hugging each other and touching players as they passed by, as if the players had some magical power that might rub off – and seeing that film it seemed as if they did. There wasn't a Screech Owl watching who didn't imagine him or herself there and part of something so special nothing else in life would ever compare.

The rink itself was huge, big as an NHL rink, with red seats and ads on the boards – sports drinks, airlines, phone companies – and the ice surface so big and square that the Screech Owls, none of whom had ever skated on an Olympic-size ice surface before, could only stare as if they were seeing a mountain or the ocean for the first time. A player could get lost out there!

The dressing rooms had shelves for the equipment, hangers and lockers for the players, and, as Nish shrieked when he saw them, "Pro Showers!" The Screech Owls' home rink didn't even have one shower. The Olympic Center had a massive shower room with stainless steel tubes running from floor to ceiling that had shower nozzles sticking out at different heights and in every direction. More like a car wash than any shower Travis had ever seen, but he could hardly wait to try them.

Before the practice, they lined up for commemorative photographs, and then, when all the pictures had been taken, Muck spoke to them. Apart from the coaches and Mr. Dillinger, whistling softly as he laid out the sweaters and socks, the players were alone in the huge dressing room, the team entirely by itself. This year Muck had put an end to parents coming in. They were "players" now, Muck had said, not "helpless infants," and the change had been profound.

Travis could still remember when the tiny dressing rooms were so crammed with parents – sometimes *both* parents – that the players could barely move. He could remember how, even after it had reached a point where their sole job was tightening the skates, the parents would stay for the coach's speech, and how some of the dads

– Mr. Brown had been the worst of them – had insisted on adding their own speeches, the kids all sitting there secretly giggling and paying not the slightest attention to whatever came after the first "Listen up!"

"I want to speak to you for a minute," Muck began, his voice so soft he could have been speaking one-on-one to any of them. "This is a good tournament. We're going to have to be at the top of our game if we're going to go anywhere in it. You already know some of the teams here. We've played the Toronto Towers before. We know them and they know us. Rest assured the others are every bit as good, if not better."

Travis hated the Towers. Chippy and arrogant – the Screech Owls had played them twice before and lost once and won once. The game they won the Towers had protested, claiming Muck had stacked his team. He hadn't, of course, and the organizers had thrown the protest out. But that was the kind of team they were.

"There are teams here from New York State, Maine, Connecticut, Massachusetts, and Minnesota.

We haven't seen any of them. And the first team we play – the Portland Panthers – are the top-rated team in New England."

"We'll wipe 'em," Nish said.

Muck looked up from his piece of paper and fixed his gaze on Nish, who reddened.

"You're going to be hearing there are scouts in the stands," Muck said.

Scouts! NHL scouts watching the Screech Owls? Why?

"Some of your parents have already informed me that this is so, but I want you to understand exactly what it means. They've been there before, only you never knew about it. And I certainly never would have mentioned it to your parents.

"They are *not* NHL scouts, no matter what some of your moms and dads may be thinking. They're mostly coaches, and a few general managers of bantam teams. Maybe the odd midget team. But that's all they are. This is a convenient place for some of them to see what's coming up in their own district – and remember that, you're all committed to the Central District until at least midget age – and maybe to get a sense of how the players are coming along in other hockey areas.

"That's it. It's that simple. Nobody's going to walk up to you and say, 'Sign here and you're Evengi Malkin's left-winger for next season' . . ."

Nish let the air he'd been holding snort through his nose. Travis was surprised to find that he too had been sitting there with breath held, almost afraid to breathe. Yet Muck had been talking as calmly as if he were sitting around the dinner table, nothing more.

". . . I'm dead serious, ladies and gentlemen. I'm going to say something to you that sounds like the exact opposite of what I've been yelling at some of you now for more than four years. 'Keep your heads *down*.'"

Muck paused, letting the line sink in. "Anyone know what I mean by that? You, Travis?"

Travis tried to speak but nothing came out. He had to clear his throat and start over. "It means we should concentrate on what's going on on the ice."

"You got it. Forget the stands. Forget thinking about what might happen five or six or seven years from now. For all you know, you might be in the same jail cell as Nish here by then."

Nish sat back as everyone laughed, shaking his head in disgust, used to Muck's cracks, enjoying the moment as much as anyone but determined never to show it.

"The Screech Owls are here to play hockey – nothing else. You've heard me say it a million times. 'Hockey is a game of mistakes.' Let's not make our first one before we even leave the dressing room. Now let's go out and make a team of ourselves. Nish, you bring the pucks."

# 5

"I'm gonna hurl!"

Nish had turned his third color since morning. Red-faced and angry when the other boys had jumped on him to get him up, then white and drained by the end of the practice, he was now almost gray. Travis sat beside him in the twisting, groaning van and wondered if he should try to comfort his friend, or wisely move to the seat behind so he wouldn't get splashed if Nish indeed threw up, as he was threatening.

"I'm really gonna hurl!"

Nish wasn't alone in feeling woozy. Practice had gone so well, Muck had told them when it was over and they were dressing, that he was going to take them all up Whiteface Mountain. The Screech Owls had gone in convoy, the big van followed by a half-dozen cars, and the group had snaked in such an impossible series of rises and hairpin turns that, a couple of times, those leading in the big van could look down, way down through the trees, and see one of the following cars seemingly going in the opposite direction.

Mr. Dillinger was driving, and he seemed to be enjoying it. Every hairpin turn he would shout out "I'm losing it!" and some of the players, on cue, would scream – but they all knew he was kidding, not about to crash.

They had to drive about four miles to rise just one, through deep woods and then pine and shrub. Every turn produced a new view, but Willie Granger, who had shut his eyes after the first rise, never saw one of them. "What's the *Guinness* record for being afraid of heights?"

Wilson Kelly teased. Willie didn't let on that he'd heard.

Finally they reached the parking area near the top. They pulled up as close to the castle-shaped restaurant as they could get, parked and locked the cars, and then headed into the tunnel for the long walk to the elevator. It was dark and damp and they could hear and see water running below the walkway.

"Geez, is it ever cold!" Nish shivered.

"*toDSah!*" shouted Data, the strange word echoing. No one knew what it meant, except that it was a Klingon swearword, of which Data had dozens: *petaQ, taHqeq, ylntagh, Qovtatlh, va . . .*

"It's like a dungeon!" Sarah shuddered.

"I'm outta here!" Willie cried before they had gone ten steps. He ran back out of the tunnel.

"Wait for me!" shouted Nish.

"*va!*" barked Data, following.

"Me, too!" yelled Mario, chasing after the rest.

"Where're they going?" Travis asked, turning to watch his teammates as they flew back down the tunnel.

Mr. Dillinger was right behind him. "They'll take the stairs up," he said. "We'll take them on the way down. I can't blame them for wanting out of this."

The old cage elevator creaked and shuddered as it traveled up the inside of the mountain, the guide quietly reading a paperback as she pushed the button for the top and waited, one hand on the button, the other on her book. What a gloomy place to spend the day, thought Travis. He hoped the book had lots of action, and was set outside somewhere sunny and warm.

A few minutes later they emerged onto the observation deck, the sun like a long-lost friend when it fell on Travis's face. After a minute of feeling blinded, he got his vision back, the bright sky giving way to an unbelievable scene spreading out as far as Travis could see: blue lakes, green forest, a haze in the distance making the far hills seem almost ghostly.

There was another guide on the deck, and he pointed out the Montreal skyline far to the north, and Lake Placid and Mirror Lake and the town of Lake Placid down below, the lakes so small at this height they seemed puddles, the town all but invisible through the light haze in the air.

The players and parents broke off into little groups, most of them heading back toward the elevator, the easiest route back to the parking lot. Some wandered off on their own, taking photographs of each other and pointing out sights, before heading toward the trails and stone steps which led back down the mountain.

Travis wandered off on his own back up to the observation area. For a while he watched "Captain Video" – Norbert Philpott – and his father arguing about the correct way to film the landscape on their new camera. It was a ridiculous scene, the two Philpotts fighting for control of the new toy. Maybe they were going to wait until they got it back home and on their television before they'd enjoy the scenery.

At the far ledge, he caught up to another group, Sarah, Dmitri, and Derek, who were pumping quarters into the pay observation binoculars and trying to see Montreal more clearly, some sixty-two miles away.

"Where is the Forum?" Dmitri wanted to know.

"You can't see it," Sarah told him. "But you can see the mountain."

"I thought we were on the mountain," Dmitri said, confused.

"The Montreal mountain, Mount Royal," Sarah explained impatiently. "It's just called 'the mountain.' It's really a hill."

"Well, why don't they call it a 'hill' then?" Dmitri wanted to know.

Travis took a look, the haze so dense at such a distance he could not even tell where the mountain – or hill – was. His vision suddenly went black as time ran out and the viewfinder closed. He started fishing in his pocket for another quarter.

"Here, you kids need some change?"

They turned and Mr. Brown, grinning from

ear to ear, was marching toward them with a mittful of quarters held out.

Sometimes Mr. Brown was a bit much, Travis thought. Always offering to help out with the driving or the practices or the phoning, but pushy about it. He was always the loudest in the stands. He was always the one ripping into the officials. He'd been the only parent to argue with Muck when Muck made the decision that the team no longer needed parents cluttering up the dressing room. Mr. Brown had claimed that he, and only he, could do Matt's skates the way Matt needed them done. Muck had told him Matt could do his own skates from now on, and would learn to like them. Matt not only had done his own skates fine, he seemed much happier and more talkative since his father had ceased speaking for him.

"No, we've seen enough, thanks," said Sarah.

"Okay, okay. Just trying to help."

The kids all thanked him. Mr. Brown wasn't through.

"Look, I'm glad to catch you four here alone. You're our set-up men – sorry, Sarah, set-up *players*

– and if you guys are going, the whole team's going. And if Matt finally gets off his duff and scores a power-play goal, it's going to come from one of you. So I got a little proposition, just between us, okay?"

No one said anything. No one knew what to say.

Mr. Brown reached into his pocket and pulled out a massive roll of bills held together with a silver clip. Travis had never seen so much money at one time. On the outside was a twenty-dollar bill. If all the bills were that big, there must be a thousand dollars!

But they weren't. Mr. Brown eased the clip and spread the bills like a fan, the twenty covering another twenty, a fifty, and then a couple of tens, a few fives. Still more money than any of the kids could count at a glance.

"You guys play the way I know you can all play and I'm good for two dollars a point, okay?"

He looked at them all, one by one. They looked back, uncertain, not feeling right.

"We'll tabulate at the end of every match,

okay? I'll keep the stats, you guys keep the cash." Mr. Brown chuckled at his little joke. No one else laughed.

"Are we on?"

Travis didn't know what to say. Dmitri would not say anything: he would wait for one of the others to take the lead. Derek was staring hard at the money. That left Sarah.

"I don't think so," said Sarah, and turned abruptly away.

Her comment so caught the group off guard that no one knew what to do next. Mr. Brown seemed flustered, angry. He held the bills out once more and shook them, trying to tempt them.

"We'd better not," said Travis. "It wouldn't be fair to the other kids on the team."

"They wouldn't want to see *goals*? C'mon –"

"We'd better not," Travis repeated. "Thanks all the same."

Red-faced, Mr. Brown slapped the bills together again and rode the clip over them, then stuffed the cash in his pocket. He was shaking his head.

"It's not like I'm offering you something for *not* scoring," he said, indignant.

"We know," said Travis. "It's just that we'd better not."

The group broke up quickly, Mr. Brown heading back into the souvenir shop, the kids off and away to the next lookout area.

But Sarah was gone. When Travis next saw her, she was in the snack shop, sitting with a Coke while Muck sat, with nothing, tapping his fingers on the surface of the table.

Muck was listening. He had a look on his face like bunched-up tape. Travis didn't need to hear to know what Sarah was telling the coach.

Travis's wristwatch said 1:57. The van was to leave at 2:00 p.m. sharp, and he knew he'd be in big trouble if he was late. He'd gone out along the rock cut and lost track of the time when he came across a friendly chipmunk so used to people that he'd scrambled up onto Travis's cupped hand, up his sleeve, over his shoulder, and down into his vest pocket. From the sound of the scolding, the chipmunk had expected the pocket to be filled with nuts. Travis had then gone off searching for pine cones for the little chipmunk, and in looking had forgotten the hour. And now he had to run.

The elevator was headed down and would take far too long to come back up, so he began to run down the stone steps, skipping and jumping to the irregular shapes. Travis had to watch himself to make sure he didn't trip, but he also had to make time, and he was practically airborne when, coming from the pines, he caught the distinct voice of Muck. An angry Muck.

Travis slowed instinctively. Slightly off the trail and through the pines he could make out Muck and another man's back. From the bald spot he knew immediately it was Mr. Brown.

"And don't you ever, *ever* let me catch you doing something like that again or you'll never come anywhere near any team I run, no matter whether your boy is on the team or not. Understand me?"

Mr. Brown was rattled, upset, uncomprehending. "C'mon, Muck. It's hardly like they're getting paid to *throw* games. Where's the harm in a tiny little reward for good play? The NHL pays bonuses, for heaven's sake."

Muck began speaking very distinctly, his words short and clipped, a sure sign, as all Screech Owls knew, that his temper was boiling over.

"The 'harm,' Mr. Brown, is that you're teaching selfishness. You pay them to score, what am I supposed to do? Pay the others to back-check? Give Boucher a five-dollar bill if he makes a save? This is a *team* sport, mister."

Now Mr. Brown was angry: "You don't have to speak to me like that."

"Fine, then!" Muck snapped, biting off his words. "I won't speak to you at all."

Muck turned, leaving Mr. Brown sputtering and fuming. Mr. Brown's hands were by his sides, furiously clenching and unclenching. "Jerk!" Mr. Brown cursed, but so quietly Muck was already out of earshot.

Travis ducked back in behind the pines and took one of the other paths leading down to the restaurant and parking lot. They hadn't seen him. And the van was still there, Mr. Dillinger at the wheel waiting for the signal from Muck to go. Travis had made it in time, thanks to the heated discussion between Muck and Mr. Brown, but Travis couldn't find it in himself to be grateful to the two men. He hadn't liked the tone of the conversation. He hadn't liked at all the way Mr. Brown had stood there making fists and cursing as the coach walked away.

# 6

Travis woke with the sun on his face. He lay blinking for a while, then shifted out of the direct light of the window and lay for a while longer staring at the beam of light that seemed somehow solid and filled with hundreds of tiny, floating dust particles.

He had no idea what, if anything, could have stirred the particles up. The boys had settled down shortly after Nish gave up trying to figure out how he could rewire the television so he could finally see an adult film – "I gotta get some tools," he kept saying, "gotta get some tools" – and all had fallen asleep quickly. Travis had even managed to be last into the bathroom, which allowed him to "forget" to turn off the light again.

There was sound in the hall. People were talking, laughing, excited. But Travis couldn't make it out. Nish rolled over, grunting, and pulled a sheet up over his head, uncovering his body. His feet wiggled for blanket warmth but could find none. He sat up.

"Wazzat?" Nish asked.

Travis's mom had often told him at breakfast his eyes were still full of sleep. But Nish's whole face was still full of sleep, as twisted as the sheets, one eye stretching open and the other stuck shut, as if he had Scotch-taped himself to sleep rather than dozed off quietly the way Travis and Wilson and Data had. Nish's stuck eye popped open so suddenly Travis expected to hear a snapping sound.

"Who's making all the noise in the hall?" Nish wanted to know.

"They woke me up!" Data called, as he, too, sat up blinking. "*jIyajbe'!*" ("I don't understand.")

"Let's get dressed and go see," Travis suggested.

It was worth getting up for; even Wilson made it in time. The recreation area downstairs was filling with guests, some of the younger ones still in pajamas, all talking and pointing, some laughing and some very much upset. There were workers with pails and towels standing around the far corner of the pool where the Jacuzzi was completely hidden behind a huge, still growing cloud of soap bubbles. The bubbles were spreading onto the pool and beginning to drift across the water. The workers were trying to find the control button amid the suds so they could turn off the hot tub and stop the swirling that was only making more and more bubbles. They were not having much luck.

Norbert Philpott came running to tell the four roommates what was happening as they arrived. "Someone dumped laundry detergent into the Jacuzzi!" Norbert shouted. He had his father's new camera.

There were men in business suits running around and looking very annoyed. Several women with gold hotel badges stared at the youngsters from the hockey teams as if they'd all been in on it. The Screech Owls were one of four teams booked in the hotel. Several members of one of the teams – the Portland Panthers, Travis knew, since two of the kids had Panthers T-shirts on, – were laughing and pointing, much to the fury of one of the hotel women who was scowling directly at them.

One of the workers emerged from the bubbles with three opened soap boxes, the tiny ones from the machine in the laundry room, and held them out to some of the others as evidence.

"I bet they washed off their prints," Nish said, giggling.

But none of the adults were laughing. The men in suits and one woman with a hotel badge were huddled with Muck and three other men in sweat suits – coaches' uniforms – and all were talking very quietly, very seriously. Muck was shaking his head.

"He'll think it's me," said Nish.

"Was it?" Travis asked.

"Up yours."

Muck called the Screech Owls to the Adirondack Room for 9:30 a.m. Everyone knew what it was about. Everyone also knew that the soap storm had been caused by someone else, not one of them. Another team, perhaps. An angry hotel employee. But not the Screech Owls.

Having nothing better to do, Travis and Nish showed up early, and at the top of the escalator on the way to the Adirondack Room, they came across a tearful Sarah Cuthbertson and Sareen Goupa being led into a corner by Muck and Mrs. Cuthbertson. Sarah's mother seemed very distraught.

The two girls had dark circles around their red eyes and looked as if they had been crying. Could it be that *they* had soaped the Jacuzzi? Sarah? Sareen? Nish and Travis could not believe it. The girls never goofed around. The idea of either of them even thinking of such a thing, let alone carrying it off, was too mind-boggling to consider. But why the tears? Why were they so upset?

The boys soon found out.

When everyone got into the room, Muck called order. Mr. Dillinger, looking just as serious as Muck, shut the big doors and the place fell eerily silent, everyone waiting for Muck to speak. He seemed to start and catch himself several times, unsure of what to say.

"First off, I don't believe it was any of our team, all right?"

"Couldn't be," Mr. Dillinger said from behind the gathering.

"I don't have to tell the Screech Owls how to behave. Doesn't matter whether it's a hotel, a motel, or you're being billeted with families, you treat where you are like it's your own home. Understand?"

No one had to answer. They had heard this line from Muck since the first time they'd headed out of town for a tournament.

"I don't know who did that stupid prank and I don't much care. I know it wasn't anyone in this room. But that being said, you have to understand you're all under suspicion because I would doubt very much that those responsible are about to own up.

"I have been informed by the manager that one more incident and every one of the teams booked in here is out, no matter who's responsible. Out in the streets.

"You understand the seriousness of the situation. It doesn't matter if any of us did it or not, we do one slightly foolish thing and we may as well have done it. So be on your very best behavior from here on out."

There were mumbles of agreement from around the room. Travis was confused. None of this explained why Sarah and Sareen had been crying. It wasn't as if they had planned to spend the day in the Jacuzzi.

"We've got a bigger problem than that on this team," Muck said. He looked over at Sarah and Sareen, who were standing with Mrs. Cuthbertson, their heads down and backs slightly turned so no one would see their red eyes.

"These two young women say they were awake all night long. Pizza deliveries coming to the wrong door, banging on the walls, someone partying half the night."

Travis thought he saw Muck's gaze flicker sharply toward the back of the room. Travis turned. Mr. Brown and some of the other men stood there. Mr. Brown's face was red. His eyes looked little better than Sarah's. But not from crying.

"We're here to play in a hockey tournament. We're not here on vacation and we are most assuredly not here to keep young players up all night long when they need their sleep. I'd like a little more cooperation. Understand?"

Travis walked down the hill to the rink with Nish, Derek, Data, Willie, Sarah, and Sareen. The girls said they were in the south wing with parents on all sides of them; all the boys were in the west wing of the hotel, with the coaches at the end of the hall. Sarah thought there had been several parties going on, but the only parent's voice she recognized was, of course, Mr. Brown's.

"But it wasn't only him," Sareen said.

"The pizzas were worse," Sarah said. "They came three times. The last one was at four thirty in the morning! And it wasn't Mr. Brown who ordered them. We could hear him yelling at the poor guy when he went to his door."

Maybe the yelling was part of it, Travis thought. Maybe Mr. Brown was getting back at Sarah for going to Muck about the bribes.

And maybe it *was* nothing but too much noise. It had happened before at other tournaments. But usually it was other teams' parents. The Screech Owls' parents were generally pretty quiet – for hockey parents.

Travis's group arrived at the Olympic Center at the same time as the Portland Panthers, who had come down the big hill in their very own bus – no rental for them, it even had the team name and colors painted on the side.

The Panthers' coaches and managers were dumping the equipment out onto pull carts to take into the arena. The bags all matched and sported the team logo, and each had a number on it that would match a sweater and a player. Just like the NHL. The coaches and managers wore matching blue track suits with "Panthers" in bold yellow lettering across the back. They, and all the team, had blue caps with similar lettering. They looked almost professional.

Travis always felt funny running into the players from another team. He was always amazed at how big and tough the other team seemed, always bigger, always tougher, always seeming more cocky, more sure of themselves than Travis's team. He wondered if perhaps the Screech Owls appeared the same way to the Panthers. But since he knew the Owls so well, had seen most of them cry at some time, afraid at others, he didn't see how that could be possible. How could the Screech Owls scare another team?

The Screech Owls dressed quickly, quietly, efficiently. Travis adored these moments before a big game, the way zippers sounded coming undone on bags, the way some of the players could rip shin-pad tape around their pads so quickly and loudly that it sounded like a dirt bike was coming right through the wall. He liked the sound of Mr. Dillinger filling water bottles, the sound of old tape coming off a stick and new tape going on.

Travis divided players into two groups: those who taped from the tip of the blade to the heel, and those who began at the heel and worked to the tip. Those who began at the heel, he believed, were sloppier and did bad jobs. Travis himself would never use a stick that had been taped heel to tip.

Mr. Dillinger taped tip to heel, the right way, and sticks taped by him were perfectly smooth, each wrap perfectly overlapping the next. Still, Travis preferred to do his own sticks, even if they didn't look quite as good.

Mr. Dillinger wasn't whistling. He wasn't

joking. Perhaps he was upset about what had happened to Sarah and Sareen. Perhaps it was just that he knew how important this first match would be against the powerful Panthers. He came into the room with a pair of newly sharpened skates in each hand, one pair for his son, Derek, the other for Dmitri, who had a thing about freshly sharpened skates. Dmitri had to have them done immediately before a game. If his skates had been sharpened the day before – even if they hadn't been used since – he would ask for a fresh sharp. And Travis thought his own thing about ringing a shot off the crossbar during the warm-up was weird.

Derek, on the other hand, rarely worried about his skates. Travis smiled to himself. Perhaps with this being Lake Placid and the Olympic arena and the Screech Owls' first *international* tournament, it was a case of the trainer being more nervous than the player – especially since the trainer was the player's father.

Muck began speaking, slowly, his words smooth and long, meaning he was relaxed and ready.

"You don't know this team. From what we can gather, they can put a lot of rubber in the net. The ones to watch are their big center, number 5, and they've got a very quick little defenseman, number 4. They move the puck around well.

"We know we can sometimes panic and run around like chickens with their heads cut off. We can't have any of that against a team like this. So we stay calm out there no matter what happens.

"We get down a couple of goals I want you to forget there's even a scoreboard out there. We play our game and it's either good enough or it isn't. Understand?"

No one had to answer. They did.

"I may have to make some line changes as we go. If I change you, it doesn't mean anything except I think you'll help us more on another combination. It doesn't mean you're hurting us where you are, understand?"

No one did. No one dared to ask. Every player thought Muck was talking directly to them. Everyone thought it meant exactly what Muck had said it did not mean – that he was worried about certain players hurting the team. Travis swallowed hard and figured everyone else in the room was swallowing at the same time.

# 7

Ten minutes into the first period, Travis understood. Muck had been talking about someone specific: Sarah Cuthbertson, Travis's center, the Screech Owls' leading scorer.

Sareen, her eyes still red and swollen, was sitting on the bench as the back-up goaltender who would only come into the game if Guy Boucher happened to get hurt. But Sarah, as always, had taken the opening face-off.

The game had begun terribly. Sarah had lost the face-off and the opposing center – number 5, big, dark-haired, and menacing – had dumped it back against the boards near his left defenseman, the little number 4 that Muck had warned them to be careful around. Dmitri hadn't listened: he lunged for the puck, hoping to tip it over the defenseman's stick and into a break, but instead the quick little defender had beaten Dmitri to the puck, slammed it off the boards, past Dmitri and Sarah and perfectly onto the tape of the big center, who had already turned and had a step on Nish. The puck reached him just as he crossed the blue line. Another few inches back or a fraction of a second slower and it would have been offside; but it wasn't, and number 5 had nothing between himself and the net but poor Guy Boucher, wiggling wildly backwards to play the angle of a long shot at the same time as he protected his crease. Guy was too slow, too late. Number 5 fired from the top of the circle, a high rising slap shot that blew past Guy as if he was flapping a wing at it. 1–0, Panthers.

Six seconds into the game and all they could think of was the score, even though Muck had told them to erase the score from their minds.

Travis couldn't remember a shorter shift. *Six seconds!* Not being involved in the play, he had hardly moved. He hadn't even shaken the butterflies from his stomach, hadn't increased his pulse or broken a sweat – and here was Muck calling them off the ice and sending out Derek's line.

They sat out three shifts, Derek's line going out twice more and the game beginning to move back onto equal footing. Once, Mr. Dillinger, in crossing toward the defensive units with a water bottle, gave Travis a gentle, encouraging pat on the arm, but Travis didn't want encouragement. He wanted Muck to call Sarah's name so they could head back out and make up for things.

"Sarah!" Muck finally barked. "And stay with your man, Dmitri."

They skated back out and Travis could hear some of the parents shouting. Dmitri looked cross, angry with Muck for seeming to put the blame on him. The face-off was to be in the

Panthers' end of the ice, and Sarah was determined not to lose this one. Twice the linesman waved her around to get her to face correctly, and each time she went back to turning sideways with her bottom hand reversed, her lower grip almost at the heel of the stick, a certain sign that she was going after the puck and it was going straight back and across to Nish for the shot. Travis thought the official might wave her out altogether and he'd have to take the face-off when, suddenly, the linesman threw the puck down so hard it bounced straight back up.

Sarah was waiting for it. She clipped the puck out of mid-air on the bounce and drew it back, as Travis had known she would, to Nish, who moved in for the shot. The dark Panther center was rushing him, though, and sliding with his pads toward the puck, so Nish, instead of hammering the puck into the pads and having it bounce out over the blue line, stepped lightly around the sliding player and rifled it around the curve of the boards so it came perfectly to Travis, who was waiting, expecting.

Travis took a moment to look. A Panther defender was rushing him and trying to poke check – a mistake – and Travis took advantage of his decision by sliding the puck between the player's outstretched stick and his skates and twisting around so he was free again, the defenseman piling shoulder-first into the boards. Travis faked a pass to Sarah at the front of the net and swung the puck back to Data, who was pinching in from the far point, and Data shot.

But the shot never came through. It hit the Panthers' little blond defenseman on the chest, bounced over Sarah's stick, and landed in empty space between the crease area and the blue line. Quick as a cat, the little defenseman gathered up the puck and sped away, with Sarah in pursuit and Travis, lost in the corner, well out of the play.

The little defenseman and the big dark center raced down the ice, the puck moving twice between them. Dmitri, caught skating the other way, could not get back. Data, having taken the shot, had fallen trying to turn hard. He scrambled back fast but not quickly enough, and was also behind the play. Only Nish was back, his skates snaking backwards almost as quickly as the two Panthers' could stride forward.

Sarah was the only Screech Owl forward in position to get back into the play. She missed her check when the puck first went off the little defender, and tried to catch him, but by the blue line Sarah was digging deep, her head down, shoulders swinging, a tired player seeming to be wading waist-deep through water rather than scooting on this magnificent, hard ice, as the two Panthers were doing.

The big center cut cross-ice, the little defenseman cutting so he went over the blue line just ahead of his teammate. Nish was dead center, expecting the crisscross, playing the pass. The little defenseman looked to pass, moved his stick to pass, and Nish gambled, going down on his knees and arms to block the pass that never came. The little defenseman tucked the puck perfectly back in on his skates and kicked it niftily around the sprawling Nish, the two Panthers now home free on Guy Boucher.

Guy, caught in an impossible two-on-none situation, had no choice but to play the shot. But to do so, he had to leave the far side of the net wide open for an easy tip-in. Number 4 faked a shot, passed quickly, and big number 5 swept it into the net effortlessly.

Panthers 2, Screech Owls 0.

Two shifts, two goals-against for Sarah, Dmitri, and Travis. They didn't even have to look for Muck's hand signal to know they were coming off. All three skated over, heads down, knowing they were in trouble.

But Muck wasn't angry. When Sarah sat down he came up behind her, placed a towel around her neck, and leaned down and whispered into the earhole of the helmet. Travis couldn't hear a word. He could only, out of the corner of his eye, catch Sarah choking back tears and nodding in agreement. Muck straightened up, tapped Sarah affectionately on the shoulders, and then went first to Travis and then to Dmitri.

"We're going to mix the lines. You're on with Derek for the rest of the game."

Travis felt terrible for Sarah. She was too exhausted to play. The lack of sleep and crying had worn her down. Muck had done the right thing. Sarah would play a few shifts with the other lines, but the scoring they so desperately needed now would have to come from Travis and Dmitri and Derek, who was as good a replacement as the team had for Sarah. Muck had done what he had to do, and Muck – perhaps alone – didn't think the game was lost.

Travis and Dmitri were well used to Derek. They had played together on the odd power play and in the rare situations when Sarah would get a penalty and Travis and Derek would be sent out to kill it off. They had also worked together in a tournament at Christmas time when Sarah was off with her other team at the Canadian Women's Nationals.

Derek wasn't as smart with the puck as Sarah, but he was better at face-offs and had probably the team's best backhand. He couldn't pass as well as Sarah, but all that meant was that Travis and Dmitri would have to take the puck off their skates once in a while rather than feeling it click perfectly onto their tape, as was so often the situation with the magical Sarah.

The tournament games were set up in two twenty-minute periods, with a break, but no flood, in between. The score was still 2–0 at the break. The Screech Owls had yet to get a goal, but at least they were now holding their own. And no one was working harder than Derek Dillinger, who had stepped in so well for Sarah. He worked as hard coming back as going down, and several times had got back to break up Panther rushes. Other Screech Owls were working hard to pick up the slack. Mario, Zak Adelman, Jesse Highboy – all playing their hearts out. But what the team needed now were some good scoring chances.

"It's coming, it's coming," said Muck, who seemed much relieved at the break. Mr. Dillinger was busy making sure everyone had fresh water and a towel. Travis was standing, face-mask up, helmet half off, beside Derek when Mr. Dillinger came by with water, and he saw a proud Mr.

Dillinger quickly reach out and gently pinch Derek's arm as he passed. Nothing more, nothing that anyone but the father and son would notice. Travis felt happy for them both.

"Derek," Muck said. Derek pulled the towel off his face, staring and waiting. "You guys have got to use the fast break more. Use Dmitri's speed on right. They're lining up across the red line. You should be able to chop one off the boards that Dmitri can catch up to on-side and be in behind them. Okay?"

"Okay."

"And another thing, Travis, I want to see the third guy coming in late for rebounds, understand?"

Travis nodded. He understood.

The second period began quite differently from the first. Derek won the face-off and sent the puck back to Nish, Nish lazily circling back into his own end to draw in the Panthers' forwards. One darted for him, and Nish bounced the puck back off his own boards so the player flew past and the puck came back out to Nish, alone. He called this play his "Drew Doughty," and much to everyone's surprise, it usually worked.

Nish used the open ice to hit Derek with a pass as Derek skated toward him at the Screech Owls' blue line, and Derek niftily dropped a pass to himself as he turned, so the puck was waiting for him when he came around and headed up-ice. Travis inhaled deeply – it was a dangerous move if a defenseman was around, but as Muck had said, the Panthers' defenders were dropping back to the red line, protecting their lead.

Derek barely looked for Dmitri. He slapped the puck so it hit the boards waist-high directly in front of the Panthers' bench. The puck jumped and lost velocity and fell near the Panthers' blue line, quickly losing speed as it crossed ahead of any players.

Dmitri already had the jump on the defense. He had come out of his own corner full-steam, and Dmitri at top speed with a puck to chase was about as fast as Travis had ever seen a peewee player. He turned the Panthers' left defenseman so fast that the defender's skates caught on each other and he went down onto one knee, Dmitri gone by the time he recovered.

The Panthers' goaltender saw the play and raced for the puck. A mistake. He had misjudged twice: first that Derek's slapper would carry down into the Panthers' end, second that Dmitri Yakushev was just another skater coming at him. By the time he realized his mistake, it was too late. The goalie sprawled and slid, waving his stick and pads to create as large an obstacle as possible, but for Dmitri, gobbling up the puck at the blue line, it was child's play. He dipped around the goaltender and, from the top of the circle in, had an empty net.

Panthers 2, Screech Owls 1.

# 8

Travis loved the way momentum could shift in a hockey game. Equal skills, equal number of players, equal time on the clock, and yet sometimes a game could shift so lopsidedly, first one way, then the other, that it would seem as if only one team at a time had skates on. Like in his dream.

This time the momentum was all with the Screech Owls. This time he felt as if there were no skates on his feet, but instead of a nightmare it was that joyous sensation that comes only a few times a season, when your skates are so comfortable and your skating so natural that there is no awareness of where skin ends and steel begins.

Just as the first period had belonged to the Panthers, the second, and final, was going to belong to the Screech Owls. On the line's next shift, Derek again sent Dmitri up right wing, but the Panthers were prepared this time and Dmitri wisely looped at the corner and hit Derek with a return pass as Derek came across the blue line.

Derek shot from a bad angle, but was smartly playing for a rebound, and Travis, coming in late as Muck had said he should, found the puck sliding onto his stick directly in the slot area. He rifled a shot so hard he fell with the force, the puck ringing like a bell off the crossbar and high over the glass into the seats. There was a time when Travis Lindsay might have preferred this. There was a time – he figured every hockey player felt this way – when the finest moment possible in a game was when a puck would come back on edge and could be lofted high over the net where it would slap against the glass. Players in novice would sometimes get more excited by a good hoist than a goal. But no more. For the last year or so Travis had been able to shoot so well the concern was more in keeping it down than getting it up, and this time he had put it too high. This time he had blown it.

"Nice try," Muck said when the line came off. Travis would have none of it. He sat, his head bowed, his gloves tightly between his legs, waiting to get out there again.

Sarah was trying her best to play. She was being short-shifted by Muck to save her energy, and it was helping. She picked up a puck in her own end, played it off the boards to herself to beat a check, then hit Matt Brown at center, just barely avoiding a two-line pass. Matt dished it off backhand to Mario Terziano, who didn't have the speed but let a rocket go as he crossed the blue line, the puck rebounding perfectly to Matt, who walked in and roofed a backhand with the Panthers' goaltender on his back, waving his glove helplessly.

Panthers 2, Screech Owls 2.

"Allllll right!"

From the bench, Travis could hear Mr. Brown's bellow above all the other shouts in the arena. He looked over and Mr. Brown, who always walked along the first row of seats, was shaking the short glass and pounding it.

"Now put it to 'em!"

Mr. Brown was red in the face and seemed more angry than happy. Travis felt sorry for Matt at a time when he should have felt happiest for him. Matt's teammates were slapping him and high-fiving him and Travis knew that Matt was hearing his father's screams above everyone else's. Too much pressure for me, Travis thought. Poor Matt.

Next shift out, Matt Brown was pulled down from behind and, with Matt out of the play, the little Panther defenseman moved up into the play and rifled home a rebound to put the Panthers up 3–2. Mr. Brown went snaky behind the glass, crawling up it, and screaming at the referee.

*"Open your eyes!"*

The officials ignored Mr. Brown, who kept pounding the glass throughout the Panthers' celebrations and the face-off. Travis's line was out, and he could still hear Mr. Brown screaming.

*"Who the hell's paying you for this? You goof!"*

Just before the puck dropped, Travis saw the one official look up at the other and lightly shake his head and smile. They could hear. They knew. They understood perfectly who the "goof" was in this rink.

Nish blocked a shot beautifully from the little blond defenseman and hit Travis moving out of his own end. Travis could feel the puck on his stick and see more open ice than he'd seen all game.

He caught a flash out of the corner of his right eye: big number 5, charging at him. Travis slammed on his brakes, the big, dark center flying past him and crashing into the boards. Travis began skating hard again, heading cross-ice, but lost his footing from a hard slash across the outside of his shin. Stumbling, he fired the puck up along the boards toward Dmitri and then felt the stick across his back, slamming him face-first down onto the ice.

The Panthers touched the puck and the whistle shrieked. Travis, still on the ice, could hear Mr.

Brown screaming, swearing. He turned and he could see the big center pointing at him with his stick turned blade down, the message clear: *I'm going to get you.*

Travis couldn't figure out what he'd done. He'd stopped and the big center had crashed into the boards. He supposed he'd embarrassed him. Nothing more. If that was all it took to throw the Panthers' best scorer off his game, the Screech Owls had a chance.

The referee gave number 5 four minutes: two for slashing and two for cross-checking. He could have given him two for charging, as well, but the charge had missed so the referee had chosen to ignore it. Four minutes was more than enough.

Travis could feel Muck's confidence in the way he told them to stay out for the power play. Travis felt fine, not even aware of the slash or the cross-check, and he could sense time changing for him the way it always did when things were starting to go right for the Screech Owls.

It was as if everything moved in slow motion. Travis was aware of every player on the ice – even of Mr. Brown, screaming "Gooooo with it!" from behind the glass – and he could feel himself moving as he had always dreamed he would one day move. His stride fluid, his arms steady, head up, the puck with him. Dmitri once told him the Russians called this "dancing with the puck" and he knew exactly what they meant. However he tried to move the puck, it obeyed.

Travis beat two players, one on a shoulder fake and the second with a deft slip between the player's skates. He could hear the roar from the stands. He could see Derek racing for the open ice, hear Derek's stick slapping the ice as he called for the puck.

Travis hit him beautifully, Derek not even breaking stride as he slipped past the remaining defenseman and in on net. The goalie played him to go to the backhand as Derek crossed left to right in front of the net, but Derek shot on his forehand to the short side as the goalie began to move across with him, the puck blowing the netting out like a pillow before falling, the red light flashing, Mr. Brown bellowing.

"Alllllll rrrrrrrighttt!"

Panthers 3, Screech Owls 3, with two minutes to go.

The big, dark center of the Panthers hit a goal post and Gordie Griffith almost slipped one through the Panthers' goaltender's five hole, but the game ended in a tie.

The Screech Owls raced to congratulate Guy, who ripped his mask off a red, soaked, but ecstatic, face. A tie, yes, but they had come back from being down 2–0, which in some ways was as good as a win. And against what everyone said was the best team in the tournament!

Muck and the two assistants, Barry and Ty, and Mr. Dillinger came running onto the ice to join in the celebration. There were high fives for everyone. Muck slapped the back of Travis's helmet and Sarah gave him a friendly tap on the shin-pads, and Travis saw Mr. Dillinger throw a bear hug around his son. Derek deserved it. He had played brilliantly in place of Sarah.

The two teams lined up to shake hands. It was quick and almost the same as every other time – gloves tapping gloves, most players barely looking at each other, a few mumbling something like "Good game" or "Good luck" – but this time, when Travis reached number 4, the little blond defenseman of the Panthers who had played so wonderfully, he looked up.

And the little defenseman winked.

Winked, and smiled, and skated right past Travis and then off the ice, leaving Travis to skate back into the crowd of congratulating Screech Owls wondering what on earth that had been all about.

A good game? The crossbar? Sarah? The pizza deliveries? The Panthers wouldn't do something like that . . .

Or would they?

# 9

M uck made sure there would be no distrac-
tions that night. He talked to the hotel
manager and was able to arrange for a separate
room in the quieter west wing for the two girls. He
and the coaches of the other teams staying at the
hotel had the front desk cut off pizza deliveries to
that wing at 10:00 p.m. He made the girls go to
bed by 8:00 p.m.

Travis and several other members of the team
walked down the hill and onto Main Street to see

the sights. Travis, Nish, Data, Willie, Derek, Wilson, Zak, and Dmitri kept to one group and others took off in their own little groups. They were too many to stick entirely together, though some would have preferred to. Travis could never understand why some wanted to do everything as a team. He thought eight was more than enough – more than would ever be on the ice together at the same time.

Nish, of course, wanted to buy a T-shirt. He had a shirt from every tournament trip they had ever been on: Niagara Falls, Muskoka, Montreal, Ottawa, Peterborough, London – Ontario, not England. One size extra-large, and Nish was content for the rest of the trip.

His parents had given him twenty dollars to buy the shirt. It was all he had, fortunately, for if they'd given Nish a hundred he would have come back to the hotel wearing Lake Placid sweatpants, a T-shirt, wrist sweatbands, a sweatshirt with a hood, and, what he seemed to like best, a baseball cap with two big doggie doos, plastic and odorless, mercifully, perched over the brim.

If something was truly disgusting, then Nish would want it.

It was cool, Main Street feeling more as if it were down in a dark basement than high in the mountains. But the sun was set now and the only light came from the streetlights. A breeze was blowing in off the lake and seeming colder every time it rippled their jackets. Travis had his Screech Owls windbreaker on and wished he had a sweater beneath. It was strange being up this high: summer in the day, winter at night.

Nish got his T-shirt at one of the trinket shops backing onto Mirror Lake. At $17.99 Travis and the others felt he'd been ripped off, but Nish was delighted with the shirt. It had the Olympic rink and the 1980 Team U.S.A. pictured on it, and "The Impossible Dream" written above "Lake Placid, N.Y." Travis told him it looked like the T-shirt was made before Nish was born, but Nish just gave him a huge raspberry, patted the bag that was holding the shirt, and headed back out the door, mission accomplished.

He stopped at a turning display tray.

"Hey! Look at that!"

Travis and the others stopped, stared, saw nothing.

*"nuq?"* Data asked. ("What?")

Nish reached out his free hand. "This!" He had a small plastic tool kit in his hands.

"You want a toy now?" Willie asked sarcastically.

"Naw. Look at it. It's perfect!"

Everyone looked. Everyone saw a child's tool kit: screwdriver, pliers, adjustable wrench. So cheap they'd probably break first turn. All in a plastic case for $3.99.

"I could fix our TV," Nish said.

"There's nothing wrong with our TV," Travis said.

Nish looked at him, shook his head in pity. "They cut off our movies, didn't they?"

"You've never even seen one," Travis countered, defensively.

"Which is why we need these tools," Nish said, plucking the package free of the case. "C'mon, a buck apiece."

"No way," said Travis.

"I got a buck," Data said.

"I got fifty cents," said Zak.

"Me, too," said Dmitri.

Nish turned to Willie. "You in?"

"It's stupid," Willie said.

"You in?" Nish repeated.

"I guess."

They pooled their money and Nish paid. Travis felt uneasy, as if they were buying cigarettes or something else they shouldn't have. But it felt weird to be uneasy over a child's tool kit.

Travis, Nish, and the others walked up and down both sides of the street. They saw the old wooden toboggan-run down by the water. They saw the little band shell in the park. The movie theater, the dozens of T-shirt and souvenir shops, the art galleries, the arcade, the frozen yogurt outlets not yet opened for the tourist season.

Data bought a pin and, for his mom, a silver spoon saying "Lake Placid, N.Y." for her collection. Zak Adelman bought hockey cards, but the best he could come up with was a Taylor Hall that Willie, the world's expert in everything, said might be worth a lot more some day, and an Erik Karlsson that, according to some guide, was "hot."

Travis bought nothing and kept walking. He didn't bother arguing with Willie, but Travis was beginning to have his doubts about trading cards. He'd collected all through novice and atom and at the beginning of peewee, but one day he had walked into a card store and suddenly just lost interest. Simple as that. Just completely lost interest.

Travis figured he'd been spending an average of three dollars a week buying cards – usually one lousy pack! – and while he did have a hardcover collection of Mario Lemieux and Wayne Gretzky (autographed!) and Adam Oates and Teemu Selanne and Sergei Fedorov and Mike Richter and Adam Graves and Pierre Turgeon and Alexei Yashin and Radek Bonk and, of course, Bure, the favorite, he had about ten thousand cards in a big box that meant nothing to him and nothing to anyone else, either.

Besides, he'd started to wonder whether or not they were really worth anything at all. Right from the start his dad had said the whole collecting thing was "a house of cards," which, according to his mother, meant it was phony, not real, and while Travis had periodically got testy over his father's continuing cracks about the real value of cards, he was beginning to think his father might be right after all.

Just for fun, Travis had tried to sell about a half-dozen of his better cards. He picked out the autographed Gretzky, a few Donruss Ice Kings, some Ultra award winners and a Patrick Roy and Eric Lindros from the Topps Gold Series, and took them to a flea market where a number of dealers had tables set up.

"Would you like to buy these?" Travis had asked each one in turn.

And each one in turn had done exactly the same thing: taken the dozen or so cards, walked through them with their fingers, checking, and then handed every one of them back, including the Gretzky. "Don't need 'em," the dealers would say.

At first this made sense to Travis, but after a while he was wondering if, in fact, "Don't need 'em" meant "Don't want them," and that what they were really saying was that the cards weren't worth anything to them or to him. According to one guide, a Sidney Crosby card he had was worth fifty dollars, but that didn't mean you could cash it in at the bank.

He took the same cards in to the local card store, a little store run by a kind, elderly man who sometimes threw in a free card or a hardcover or, once in a while, even a free monthly *Beckett* magazine so Travis could look up the values of his cards.

"I'd like to cash these in," Travis said, handing the cards over.

The man, smiling, took the cards and examined them, just like the men had done at the flea market. "You've got some dandies here," he told Travis.

"They're worth a total of $86.50," Travis said. According to *Beckett*.

The man smiled. "I'm sure they are," he said. "But we're not buying right now, Travis."

Travis felt dizzy. Three years of buying a package a week — nearly five-hundred-dollars' worth of cards at home, and nobody "needs" them and nobody's "buying right now?"

"Tell you what," the man said. "I'll swap you these for this Fedorov group. Deal?"

Travis took the deal. But he also took the hint. Cards were worth cards; they weren't worth money. They had next to no value at all to anyone except for the kids foolish enough to hand over their allowance. From that day on, he was, at best, a casual collector. He knew now what his dad had meant when he called the whole thing "a house of cards."

*"nuqDaq Derek?"* Data asked. ("Anyone see Derek?")

The group stopped at the corner, Travis about to step off the curb. He hadn't even been thinking of keeping track of everyone. But they'd been warned by Muck to stick together when they went out. And now Derek was missing.

"Maybe he went back to the hotel," Willie suggested.

"Why would he?" Nish giggled. "I have the TV tools right here."

"This isn't funny," Travis said. "We have to find him."

They backtracked and began checking the stores they'd wandered through. No Derek. Finally Wilson pointed across the street.

"There's something we missed!" he shouted. It seemed he'd forgotten Derek. He was pointing to an arcade, the lights flashing inside. The group broke into a run, Nish causing a driver to slam on his brakes and shake a fist at him. Nish shook his fist back and made like a dog barking as the car shot by.

Derek was inside. He'd seen the lights and wandered off. And when they found him, he was so deep into a game of "Mortal Kombat" that he didn't even notice his teammates surrounding him to watch.

But that was Derek. Serious to a fault. Different from his father. Travis sometimes wondered if perhaps Mr. Dillinger had *too much* personality for Derek to deal with. Maybe he took up so much room that Derek had become a bit of a quiet loner in reaction. And yet they had in common their love of hockey. Derek worked so hard at it and Mr. Dillinger, obviously, was very proud of him. Mr. Dillinger was always kidding about when Derek would make the Leafs and how he would have free season's tickets to the Air Canada Centre.

The boys became so caught up watching Derek play they forgot they'd ever lost him. Soon Nish was bumming more money from the rest of the players so he could join in on the fun, too.

Travis had only five dollars, and he knew if he cashed it in on tokens he'd be five dollars short in about five minutes. So he held on and watched. Data had ten dollars' worth of tokens and, as usual, Nish was more than happy to borrow. They played air hockey and pool. They shot baskets. And, of course, they played video games, games so violent his mother would have marched him right out if she'd seen what they were doing to each other. At one point Nish's character hit Travis's character so hard he split in half and blood gushed all over the screen and the screen flashed, "Place token in now for extra game. Place token in now for extra game." But Nish was out of tokens.

The Screech Owls left in a group, Derek with them, and turned back down toward the hotel, prepared to call it a night. The streets were still filled with people, and Travis could tell the hockey crowd from the locals easily. The locals didn't look around. They knew where they were going. The hockey crowd was obvious: the jackets and caps, the way kids shouted across the street to each other, the way the parents awkwardly hung around in groups. Why they all felt they had to be friends when some of their children didn't even like all their own teammates baffled Travis.

He was tired and the jostling crowds were getting to him. Doors to restaurants and shops and bars were opening and closing on so many different sounds that he felt more that he was in a midway than a small town. He'd be glad to get back to his bed. He hoped Nish's cheap tools broke on the first try.

Travis was walking along only half paying

attention when, suddenly, he pitched face-first out over the curb and onto the road, a car braking and squealing as the driver yanked the steering wheel hard and away from his sprawling body.

The impact knocked Travis's breath out, so he had no voice to add to what he could hear behind him.

"What the hell was that for?" Nish was shouting.

There were other voices, unfamiliar.

"Get a life, fatso!"

"C'mon, runt! Get on your feet!"

"What's the matter? Need your *girl* here to do your fighting, too?"

# 10

Travis felt as if he'd been punched in the heart. Data hurried to him, bending down, looking concerned. Data dug in his pocket for a Kleenex and pushed it down toward Travis's eye, and when he dabbed it off Travis could see in the thin light from the streetlamp that the Kleenex was black with blood.

But there was no pain. He couldn't breathe. He had felt this kind of pain once before when, flying in behind the opposition net, his stick had somehow become stuck in a crack in the boards and the handle had rammed up into his gut on impact. He felt like he was going to die then, felt like he was going to die now.

Nish was still shouting: "What a stupid thing to do! What the hell's wrong with you?"

The other voice again, this time a little nervous: "I never did nothin'. He tripped over his own feet; you saw it yourself."

"I saw you stick your foot out, jerk!"

Data and Wilson had Travis turned over, Data dabbing with the Kleenex, Wilson pumping Travis's legs. Why do they always do that? Travis wondered. You lose your breath from your chest, and they pump your legs. Do they think people fill up like bike tires? But, pumping or not, he was already feeling better.

"You're going to need stitches," Data said. "There's a big hunk of flesh hanging out."

Now Travis could feel his head. It was like the pain was racing from his lungs to his head and arriving twice as large as when it had left. He could feel his right eye already swelling.

"You okay, buddy?"

That voice again. Travis opened his eyes and looked up, the head peering down at him lighted from behind so it seemed black and featureless. He could not make out who it was.

"Help me up," he said.

Data kept pressure on the cut. Wilson grabbed one arm and the faceless stranger the other.

"Get your hands off him jerk!" Nish shouted, trying to move in.

Travis felt himself yanked as the two fought over possession. Then he heard Data's high, shrill voice, bringing order.

"Shut up! Just everybody stand back! Come on, now! Stand back!"

All but Data and Wilson did. Travis stepped back up onto the curb and shook his head, Data's hand moving with the shake. He could see that a crowd had gathered. He could see his teammates – more than he had set out with – and he could see several vaguely familiar faces. The little blond defenseman who had winked at him was there, his hands jammed in his Panthers' jacket pockets, looking concerned. The big dark center, looking scared: yes, his had been the face peering down that Travis could not make out.

"Sorry about that, buddy," the big dark center said, his voice milky with sincerity. "Neither one of us was looking where we were going, I guess."

Nish pushed in, violently shaking his head. "That's bullroar, Trav. This yahoo stuck his foot out on purpose –"

"Did not –"

"Did so!"

"Up yours."

"Up yours, jerk."

"Quit it, now! We have to get this cut looked at, okay?" Good old Data, the high-pitched voice of reason.

Data had hold of one of Travis's arms, Wilson the other. They were trying to lead him away, but the big dark center pushed past Nish.

"Look, buddy, I'm awfully sorry about the cut. No hard feelings?"

He had his hand stuck out to shake. Nish's face, peering from behind, looked like a twisted-up sponge. "Tell him where to stick it, Trav –"

But Travis was confused. A hand offered should be a hand taken. He reached out, realizing his own hand was already shaking, and the two players made clumsy contact. The big dark Panther center was smiling, relieved.

"Sorry, okay?"

"What the hell's going on here?"

Travis knew this voice. It was Mr. Dillinger. He was pushing through the crowd, taking charge even before he had arrived. Travis was relieved to hear the familiar sound of someone who always knew the right thing to do.

"Travis Lindsay! What the dickens happened to you?"

Data explained the obvious: "He's got a cut forehead."

Mr. Dillinger moved right in, taking the Kleenex from Data and lifting Travis's chin and examining the cut under the weak light. "This'll need a couple," he said. "What happened?"

A dozen voices answered at once:

"We bumped into each other by accident –"

"– tripped on purpose –"

"– hit his head when he slipped –"

"– pushed –"

"– stupid curb –"

"Hold it!" Mr. Dillinger shouted, holding up both hands like a referee. "Travis, what happened?"

Travis probably knew least of all. His head was now screaming in pain. "I guess we accidentally bumped into each other," he said. "And I was the one who went down."

"Travis –" the voice of despair, disbelief, the voice of Nish.

Mr. Dillinger had no more interest in the story. "Come on," he said. "I'll take you to the hospital. Data, you come along to check the bleeding."

This night it was Travis's turn to get no sleep. The doctor at the emergency ward had frozen the area around Travis's cut, stitched it up, and, for nearly two hours, Travis hadn't felt a thing. Mr. Dillinger had stayed with him the whole time. Travis felt so grateful to him. Mr. Dillinger had been coming up from the rink when he'd noticed the commotion and gone across the street to check. Good old Mr. Dillinger, always on duty, always there when they needed him. Muck had let him handle the situation entirely, as usual. Muck ran the team on ice, Mr. Dillinger off.

Travis was fine at first. He had even gotten a kick out of watching, out of his one good eye, Nish desperately trying to remove the protective metal coupling from the back of the video box so he could plug the cable line directly into the television and, according to Nish's plan, watch all the forbidden movies for free. But the coupling wouldn't give. The cheap pliers broke. And by midnight Nish had given up in frustration and Travis had started to cry from the rising pain as the freezing left. He couldn't even turn into his pillow to hide the tears. Anything touching his forehead, even soft cotton, was like a coal jumping out of a campfire onto his skin.

Data called Mr. Dillinger, who came with some painkillers the doctor had given Travis, made him take two, and after a while Travis had dozed off into a half-sleep, half-stupor. He didn't even know, or care, if the bathroom light was still on.

He'd dreamed – imagined? – he finally met up with his long-lost "cousin," Terrible Ted Lindsay, and the two of them had compared stitches. Since these were Travis's first three, he was only about four hundred short of his hero, but Terrible Ted had smiled, half his teeth gone, half broken off, and told him hockey stitches were like military ribbons and that even if Travis only had three, he now had proof he had served and served well.

Travis was confused. Was he asleep? Awake? Did three stitches from falling – being pushed? – off a street curb in Lake Placid equal three stitches from a corner punch-up with Rocket Richard? He thought not. Terrible Ted, grinning from ear to lopsided ear, thought so. After all, it was a tough hockey opponent who had given them to Travis.

He dreamed his father came home from the office with news that the Simcoe Construction crew working on the town renovations had uncovered a variety store that had been boarded up after a fire in the 1950s and had somehow been completely forgotten. His father wanted to know if Travis was interested in going down with him to take a look at what they'd found.

Travis was certain it had happened: he and his father driving downtown and stopping outside a boarded-up front, the construction foreman welcoming the two of them with white hard hats the way they did whenever Travis went along with his father to a site, the big plywood coverings coming off the doors.

The lost store had looked so real: a metal cigarette sign over the door, tinted yellow plastic on the windows, a display of huge five-cent chocolate bars inside, and a tub of soaking wet, ice-cold tiny Cokes and ribbed Fanta orange drinks and tall Muskoka Dry ginger ale . . .

And there, tucked in under a glass cover that lifted up, three full boxes of Parkhurst Hockey Cards, 1956–57!

Travis's father, smiling, had handed the boxes over to Travis and Travis had ripped the cards open: Gordie Howe, two Terrible Teds, BoomBoom Geoffrion, Rocket Richard, Tim Horton, Jean Béliveau, Jacques Plante, George Armstrong . . . dozens and dozens and dozens of hard-edged, mint-condition cards packed in with even harder forty-year-old gum. How much would a Gordie Howe card be worth? A Rocket Richard? Jacques Plante? Terrible Ted? Priceless, to his cousin, Terrible Travis.

But then Travis had surfaced from this wonderful dream and gone over it carefully to see if perhaps it really had happened, and remembered that was the one season, 1956–57, when no hockey cards came out. Not only did the lost store not exist, but the cards could never have existed, even if the lost store were somehow real.

Travis felt something on his temple and brushed lightly with his hand. A tear, but from the pain of the cut or from the pain of waking up to reality, he could not tell.

All through the night he drifted in and out of weird, impossible dreams. Travis with the Stanley Cup. Travis in jail. Travis with a hippopotamus living in his back yard. Travis shot in the forehead by Nish's character from the video arcade . . .

"Rise 'n' shine, boys!"

It was Nish, first up for once. He was up and spraying them with cold water from a water pistol he'd somehow sneaked into the room. The others dove under the covers. Travis tried to dive, but his forehead hit the sheets like they were a goalpost.

"Owwww . . . Owwww, owww, owwww –"

"Hey, c'mon, Nish, not Travis!" Good old Data. Last night's nurse. This morning's guardian.

"We're on the ice at ten," Nish said, packing the pistol into his pajamas. "Let's go."

They began to get ready. Travis sat up, the pain increasing as he tried to get a grip on where he was and what had happened to him. Everything seemed fuzzy.

"Wow!" Nish shouted when he looked at Travis. "Look at you!"

Travis got up, the pain now shooting, and headed into the bathroom where he looked, blinked, and looked again, into the mirror.

The figure was somewhat out of focus, but it was him. At least it was *half* him. One side of his face looked normal, the other black and purple and swollen hideously over the eye. The eye itself was all but closed. He looked a million times worse this morning than he had last night.

"You look like Sarah," Nish called, giggling from the other room.

No way. Sarah looked in perfect shape compared to this.

# 11

"Maybe you should sit this one out."
Travis heard what Muck said but couldn't
understand why his coach was saying this. Mr.
Dillinger had taken one look at Travis's face at
breakfast, shaken his big beard from side to side,
and hurried off to consult with the coaches. Muck
and his assistants had come back, stared, touched
everywhere on Travis's face but where the stitches
were, and looked concerned.

"If the decision were up to me," said Mr.

Dillinger, "I'd say no."

Muck wasn't sure: "We'll check again just before game time."

By four o'clock the swelling had gone down considerably. Mr. Dillinger checked Travis before the rest of the players arrived and figured he'd be playing. "Couple of days from now, you won't even be able to find it," he teased.

"I want to play," Travis said.

"We need you," Mr. Dillinger said. He seemed pleased that Travis had come back so fast.

"I gotta go work on some skates," Mr. Dillinger said. "You may as well start getting dressed."

Travis was happily pulling on his underwear when Muck came in, took one long look at him and decided that Travis had better sit out the game against Duluth.

"I'm fine," Travis said. "Mr. Dillinger says the swelling will be gone in two days."

"And in two days I might need you. I won't need you tonight. But if we get into the final, I'm going to want you there. You get hit again today, even with your mask, that cut could open up again. Besides, you can barely see out of that eye."

"I can see."

"You can see well enough to watch."

Mr. Dillinger came whistling back into the room, carrying pairs of sharpened skates in each hand and under each arm. He stopped whistling when he saw Muck and Travis in deep conversation.

"Travis won't be dressing," Muck told him.

"He won't?"

"Maybe next game," Muck said, and wheeled away.

Mr. Dillinger caught Travis's eye. He shook his beard in quick disagreement. "I thought for sure you'd play, son," he said.

He seemed genuinely unhappy with the decision. Travis felt good that someone, at least, was as sure as he was that he needed to be out there if the Screech Owls were going to win.

Travis sat with the Screech Owl families and hated every second of it. When the teams came out for the warm-up he wanted to be out there ringing his good-luck shot off the crossbar. When they lined up for the opening face-off, he wanted to be out there with everyone in the building, aware that he, Travis Lindsay, number 7, was in the Screech Owls' starting lineup.

But now his place was taken by Derek Dillinger, with Sarah back at center and Dmitri on right wing. Derek was a good winger but a better center, and Travis wondered how he would fit in. He found himself half hoping he wouldn't, but then realized what he was thinking and shook off the thought. Travis's not playing had nothing to do with Derek, who was merely filling in where the coach told him to. And Derek, Travis knew, would be far happier knowing Travis was on the wing and he was back at center, even if it was second-line center.

Sarah was obviously much better rested. On the first shift, against the slower but bigger Duluth team, she picked up the puck behind her own net and skated out so fast she caught two Duluth forwards back on their heels and beat them cleanly. The Screech Owls had a four-on-three at their own blue line.

Then, in a move Travis had seen her try only in practice, Sarah did a spinnerama move past the opposing center, turning around in a full circle at full speed as the checker went for the puck and found himself skating helplessly toward his wingers who were, like him, caught badly out of position. It was now a four-on-two, with big Nish steamrolling right up center to join the play.

Sarah handed off to Dmitri, who dropped back to Nish, who hit Derek perfectly coming in from the side with the goaltender guarding against the other side, where Sarah was coming in backwards, looking for a tipped shot. Derek had the whole empty side to shoot at and he roofed the puck in off the crossbar, the ring announcing the Screech Owls' first goal and, by the reaction in the stands, the sweetest goal of the tournament.

Travis was caught between cheering wildly and burning with envy. If he hadn't fallen – *been tripped?* – it would have been him, not Derek, putting it in off the crossbar. Just as he always scored in his imagination. It would have been *him,* not Derek, they were all high-fiving, *his* number, not Derek's, that the scorers – and the scouts! – would be writing down on the sheets, *his* name, not Derek's, that would be bouncing around the arena walls from the public address system, *his* name, not Derek's, that they would be tying to this spectacular goal for the rest of the tournament.

Sarah Cuthbertson did not take the next shift of this line. Either Muck was juggling – and why would he juggle when the Screech Owls were so obviously superior? – or else something was wrong. Muck shifted Derek over to center and moved Matt Brown up onto the first line.

Travis was on the opposite side of the rink, but he could see Sarah bending down, working on her skates. He saw Sarah handing her skates back to Mr. Dillinger, who left the box with them, jumped over the sideboards and hurried down the side of the rink with the dressing-room key in his mouth and entered the dressing room. Sarah, her head down, expression hidden by her helmet and face-mask, still looked forlorn as she sat and waited.

Another shift later, Mr. Dillinger returned with the skates. They had probably just needed sharpening. Sarah missed a good part of her next shift tying them up, but made it out in time to see Derek pot his second goal, a beautiful slap shot from the point set up when Nish pinched in and Derek dropped back and Nish magically tucked the puck back between his own legs to where Derek was turning at the blue line.

On her next shift, Sarah barely made it down the ice before she was hustling back to the bench clutching her sweater out from her back and screaming something through her facemask. Again, Mr. Dillinger went to work. There now seemed to be something wrong with her shoulder pads.

She missed another shift as Mr. Dillinger worked frantically with tape to put the pads back together again. He finished, pulled her jersey down tight, and Muck sent her back out – just as the buzzer went to end the first period. The game was half over, and Sarah had one assist and, at the most, thirty seconds of ice time.

How could something so dreadful happen again to Sarah? Travis couldn't understand it. Some of the fathers were saying somebody must have cut her equipment. Mr. Brown, moving restlessly down in front of the glass, was unusually silent, studying the Screech Owls' bench for some indication of which line his son was going to be playing on for the rest of the game.

The idea that someone might have doctored Sarah's equipment seemed impossible to Travis, right up until her second shift of the second, and final, period, when Sarah came racing out from the corner, slamming her stick furiously on the ice as she headed for the bench, and Matt Brown, the sweat of double-shifting turning his sweater a different color from Sarah's, jumped over to take the left wing while Derek moved quickly to center again.

This time it was her pants. Mr. Dillinger tried tape, but tape wouldn't adjust, so he had to race, again, for the dressing room and come up with replacement braces.

Fortunately, the Screech Owls didn't seem to need her – or Travis, for that matter. Derek set Matt Brown up for a one-timer and, ten seconds later, sent Dmitri in on a break to put the Owls up

4–0. Derek Dillinger was well on his way to being chosen, for the second time in a row, the most valuable player of the game.

And all Travis could think was: It could have been me.

But no one else was moping for him. Travis looked around and could see that Sarah's parents were furious. The men along the back wall were angry and talking and shaking their heads. They hardly looked like parents of the winning side.

Down along the glass toward the other side, Travis could see several members of the Panthers standing watching. The little blond defenseman was there, as well as the big dark center. The Panthers were on the ice next. The big dark center was pointing at Mr. Dillinger struggling with Sarah's braces, and he was laughing.

Travis couldn't help but think that these laughing Panthers had something to do with what was happening. But what? And how?

"Someone cut it. You can see for yourself."

Mr. Dillinger was surrounded by a large crowd of parents, tournament officials, other coaches, and Screech Owl players. He had the laces he had replaced, the shoulder pads, and the braces for the pants, all cleanly sheared for a bit, then torn.

"Whoever did it knew what they were doing," Mr. Dillinger continued. "Nothing broke while she was dressing, but as soon as enough stress was put on it on the ice, everything started snapping."

"Who had access to the equipment?" a man in a suit asked.

Muck answered. "Coaches and manager. Players if they wanted, but no players came around."

"You kept all your equipment at the rink?" the man asked.

"Everything," Muck said. "We were assigned one of the figure-skating rooms across from the dressing rooms."

"Locked?"

"Of course locked."

"And no idea who?"

"No idea at all."

Travis wondered if perhaps he should talk with Muck about the Panthers, but what would he say? That one of them had winked at him during the first game when Sarah couldn't play? That some of them were laughing during the second game when Sarah couldn't play? That one of them had made a crack about Sarah during the scuffle last night?

When Travis tried to make sense of it, he could make little, but he could see why the Panthers might want Sarah out of the way. If they had got her out of the first game then they would have had a chance to grab first place right from the start and could probably have hung onto it for the rest of the tournament. On the final day, first and second place would play in the final, with the gold medal going to the winner and silver to the loser. Teams coming third and fourth in the standings would play off for the bronze, just like in the Olympics.

It made some twisted sense for the Panthers to get Sarah out of the Screech Owls' second game as well. If the Screech Owls had somehow lost, with only one point from their first-game tie, the Owls might well have been eliminated at that point from playing in the final. This would have meant the Panthers would end up playing one of the weaker teams for the championship. Crazy, but possible.

Travis decided he would talk to Mr. Dillinger. He had a chance when everyone else was still showering and dressing and Muck had gone off with the tournament officials to discuss what they should do about the situation.

Mr. Dillinger listened carefully while Travis stumbled through his confusing explanation about the cut equipment. He was no longer the laughing, kidding guy Travis had come to expect. Mr. Dillinger was dead serious.

"You're talking sabotage," he said when Travis was finished.

"What's that?"

"Deliberate. They'd sabotage in order to win the tournament."

"I guess."

Mr. Dillinger considered this for a long moment. "Makes some sense, Travis," he said, finally. "Makes some sense."

"What can we do about it?"

"Well," Mr. Dillinger said thoughtfully. "We've obviously got no proof and we'd need proof. Why don't you and some of the guys keep an eye out on the Panthers, particularly that guy who dumped you last night, and see if maybe they say something or do something that gives us a lead."

"Spy on them?"

Mr. Dillinger laughed, the old Mr. Dillinger back. "Not 'spy' – watch. Just watch them if you see them around the rink. And tell me or Muck if you see anything suspicious."

"Okay."

"Good."

# 12

The swelling around Travis's eye was going down quickly. He could see clearly again by evening, and the color was now more like that of a bad orange than a threatening thundercloud. Even the stitched area was tightening and shrinking. It was wonderful to have stitches when they no longer hurt. He felt closer to Terrible Ted than ever.

Travis and Nish had called the players together in the afternoon to discuss what was going on with the sabotaged equipment. Later on, there was to be a parent get-together, a mid-tournament party that Mr. Dillinger had set up when he booked the rooms, and Nish and Data and Derek had already helped Mr. Dillinger carry several cases of beer from the van into the Skyroom at the back of the Holiday Inn. The players knew that the main topic of conversation for the parents would be the same one the kids were meeting to discuss.

The players met by the Jacuzzi, now clean and clear and watched periodically by a nasty-looking woman from the front desk. Nish and Travis and Data set up the pool chairs around the hot tub, which, for once, wasn't full of parents, the kids turned off the noisy bubbles, and Travis, much to his own surprise, pretty well carried the meeting.

He detailed what he knew about the Panthers. He told them everything he had already told Mr. Dillinger. The wink. The laughter. The trip. The obvious fact that Sarah stood between the Panthers and the tournament victory.

"Ridiculous," Sarah said when Travis was finished.

"No," Nish argued. "It makes sense."

"You're saying they were the ones sending the pizzas."

"Yeah."

"And the ones who cut my laces and straps."

"Yeah."

"No way. No kid would ever do something like that."

Travis butted in: "Their big center would. He's got a mean streak."

"And what about the little defenseman?" Data added. "What'd he wink at you for?"

"Because he fell in *loooove* with Travis!" Wilson shouted. Everyone laughed.

"Who could fall for something that looks like *that*?" Sarah teased.

"*blmoHqu'!*" said Data. ("You look very ugly.")

Everybody laughed again. Travis was falling in love himself: with his stitches.

"It makes sense," said Nish.

"It only makes sense because we don't know what happened," countered Sarah.

"Well," Nish said, his back up, "you tell us what you think happened, then."

"I don't know." Sarah stopped for breath. She seemed on the verge of tears. "I just . . . want it to stop."

"So do we all," said Travis. "That's why we're talking about what to do. I think we should set up a watch."

"A watch?" Wilson asked.

"We should keep an eye on the room where the equipment's stored."

"We can't," Gordie Griffith offered. "We've got a ten o'clock curfew. They'd never let us stay up and they'd certainly never let us stay out at the rink."

"We'll record it!" Norbert shouted.

"What?" a half-dozen of the Screech Owls asked at once.

"Record it," Norbert said, suddenly totally assured. "My dad has his new camera here. I can rig it up on a timer."

"You mean set it up in the equipment room?" Nish asked.

"Sure. Then, if anything screwy happens, we'll see it when we play it back."

"Won't work," Gordie said, certain.

"Yes, it will," Norbert countered, equally sure.

"You'd need lights."

"No way. This new one takes available light. No flash, nothing. It can pick up things in the day you can't see. You shoot outside at nine o'clock at night, it looks like noon."

"That's true," Wilson said. "I've seen it."

"But how would we set it up?" Sarah asked, ever practical.

"Yeah," Nish added, suddenly giving up. "How can we get in?"

"There's still a game on," Travis said. "We can get into the rink."

"But what good's that do us?" Nish asked. "The equipment's under lock and key."

"Oh yeah," Travis said, now as disheartened as his friend.

Derek Dillinger cleared his throat. He didn't usually say anything when there were more than three or four others around. "I can get the key," he said.

"You can?" Nish asked.

"My dad's going to be running the bar at the parents' get-together. The keys will be in our room. I can get them."

The kids all looked at Derek with new respect. Finally, Travis spoke for everyone.

"Let's do it."

They decided that only some of them would go on the mission. Derek had to go because he had the key. Norbert had to go because he had the camera. Travis went, and so did Nish, Data, Willie, Sarah, and Wilson. They had no trouble getting into the rink. As players, all were wearing tournament pins that allowed them to come and go as they pleased. And no one thought anything of a bunch of kids coming into a hockey game as a group, one of them carrying a camera.

"You fellows on a scouting mission?" the elderly gentleman at the front desk asked.

"You bet," Nish answered, giggling.

The gatekeeper waved them through. They headed into the rink area where a game was under way: the Panthers versus the Toronto Towers. Everyone had figured the Towers would be one of the dominant clubs at the tournament, but the Toronto team was already down 5–2 with time still to run in the first period. The Panthers scored again as the Screech Owl players came out into the stands at the far end. With the parents behind the Panthers' bench stomping and blowing on plastic horns, the little blond defenseman was being mobbed by his teammates at center ice, the big dark center high-fiving him as the others rapped his helmet and slapped his back.

"Perfect timing," announced Nish. "They're probably planning a raid right after the game."

"I still don't think it's them," said Sarah.

The Screech Owls watched to the end of the first period. Then, with the people in the stands heading for the snack bar and the teams huddling at their benches, the Owls casually walked out through the dressing-room doors, with no one paying them the slightest attention.

Data raced ahead and set up a watch. At the far doors, he signaled back with his hand for the rest to go ahead. They checked for the equipment storage room they'd been assigned on arrival – the men's figure-skating dressing room, which was not being used during the tournament. The rooms had small windows on the big orange steel doors, and from the light of the corridor they could see their logo – The Screech Owls – where Mr. Dillinger had taped it during the team's first practice.

Derek yanked the keys out of his pocket and quickly opened the door. The players slipped in.

Data flicked on the lights and they came on in stages, the room dimly taking shape, then coming brilliantly alive. It hurt Travis's black eye at first, but his pupils soon adjusted and the pain vanished.

Their room was in perfect order, just as they would expect from Mr. Dillinger. They quickly checked what they could: Sarah's straps, skate laces, sticks, the equipment of a few other key players, including Travis's, which made him glow with pride, and then decided everything was fine.

"What about the camera, though?" Nish asked.

"Anybody comes in here it's the first thing they'd see."

Norbert had an answer. "We place it under the bench, low, out of sight and in the dark. Then I tilt it to catch anything near Sarah's stuff. No one will ever see it."

"Will they hear it?"

"Runs dead silent."

"What about the battery? How long will it run?"

"Nothing to worry about," Norbert said. He pulled a small black attachment out of his windbreaker pocket. "This is an automatic activator. After I set it and we leave, it activates after a thirty-second delay. Any movement and it instantly turns the camera on – no lights, no sound. It's used for wildlife photography."

"So if anything happens," Sarah said, "the camera will catch it?"

"You got it."

Travis liked what he heard. "Set it up," he said. "We have to clear this place."

Norbert moved with an efficiency they never saw on the ice. He set the camera on a special holder and adjusted everything and checked the lens and set up the special activator. Satisfied, he stepped back.

"Perfect," he announced. "Now let's get outta here. We've got thirty seconds."

Travis first peeked out the door and down the corridor, where Data was still keeping watch. Data gave him the all-clear sign and Travis waved everyone out after him. Derek shut the door and locked it.

"How could they get in without a key?" Nish hissed.

"Maybe they have a master," said Wilson.

"Maybe some of the keys are the same," said Derek.

"Maybe they do it when Mr. Dillinger's around working," suggested Norbert.

"Maybe no one's getting in at all," said Sarah,

still doubting that anything so diabolical could be happening at a simple hockey tournament.

Hers was an opinion of one. The others were absolutely certain there was something bad going on, and that, somehow, the Panthers were involved.

# 13

The players knew they had to get back before Muck's curfew. They wanted to be back and in their rooms, perhaps even in bed, so there would be no questions about where they had gone and what they had been up to. Nish wanted to get back to try out his newest set of pliers. He had promised that tonight would be the night when he would finally solve the wiring mystery of the blocked television channels.

The players raced out of the Olympic Center

and up the hill toward the hotel, where they could slip in the side door leading out onto the tennis courts and the parking lot, undetected. Or so they thought.

As the players hurried up the grassy slope onto the paved area, they rose out of the dark into an unexpected scene. The parking lot was alive with people. And not just people, but their people. Several of the fathers. A few mothers. Muck. The assistant coaches. All standing in a circle, the tension coming off the circle in waves.

The players quickly ducked down in the dark and lay flat, their heads barely above the paved ledge where the sloping lawn ended and the parking lot began. It was difficult to make out the faces, but there was no mistaking that one of the men, one slightly off from the circle, was Mr. Brown. He had something out – a handkerchief – and was dabbing at his nose, which appeared to be bleeding. Travis could make out Muck in the center of the gathering.

They could hear Mr. Brown perfectly, his loud voice clearer in a parking lot on a still night than in an arena with all the echoes and other sounds. "I can damn well speak to whoever I want, whenever I want —" His voice sounded thick.

"He's drunk," Nish hissed in Travis's ear. Nish was right, Travis thought. He was glad Matt hadn't gone to the rink with them. How embarrassing it would be for him to see this. He hoped Matt was up in his room, already asleep.

Muck was speaking. It was more difficult to hear him, but they caught the tone: quiet, sure, disapproving. It was a voice they had all heard when they'd acted up on the road. But they were kids.

"It's not any of your damn business —" Mr. Brown began again.

Muck cut him off. Still soft. But completely in command. Muck's steady voice that held for no arguing back, the voice of confidence, never rising, never falling, never changing. The voice of their coach.

"You son of a —!" Mr. Brown suddenly lunged. Muck braced himself, but Mr. Brown never got through. Several of the other fathers were stepping in, blocking.

"Muck's right, you know," one of them said. Travis was certain it was Mr. Cuthbertson.

"We've all felt the same way," another said.

"You've had your say, now go to bed," said a third.

Mr. Brown seemed to shrug, then turned away toward the door. He was not walking steadily, but whether it was because of the beer or whatever had caused his nose to bleed, Travis couldn't tell. He was still muttering when he reached the door, but they could not make out much of what he said apart from the swear words.

Those in the circle waited until he was gone. One of them lighted a cigarette, the match's flare lighting his face briefly. It was Mr. Boucher. Travis considered him one of the fairest parents and knew he would help Muck if there was any trouble.

"Let's go back in," Muck said. "We've a party to wrap up."

"Good idea," Mr. Boucher agreed.

The cigarette flicked through the night toward the boys, sparking as it struck the pavement, and then skidding like a burning race car almost to the ledge.

"It's mine!" Nish hissed.

But no one else was interested. The moment the door into the Skyroom closed again Nish bolted for the smoldering cigarette and the others all asked the same question at once: "What was *that* all about?"

Travis said nothing. He thought he knew. But he wasn't sure. The players raced for the door in order to beat the parents to the rooms. Travis could hear Nish behind him, coughing violently.

Nish was first up in the morning. When Travis woke, Nish already had the television turned around backwards and was busily prying off the protective coupler that joined the cable line to the pay-TV box. He was whistling while he worked, the way Mr. Dillinger sometimes whistled when he was happily sharpening skates.

"I think I've got it," Nish said.

"Got what?" Travis wanted to know. Or maybe he didn't want to know.

"If I can get this cable off here and attach it down there, it should work directly through the TV. Won't even have to run it through the box."

Travis didn't follow. Groggily, he pulled the cover off his bed and up onto his head like a hood and wiggled to the edge of the bed to watch.

Nish had his tools laid out like a master workman. He had the protective coupling pulled back and had slid it up over the cable so it was well back and out of the way. He was twisting the connector off the pay-TV box. The television picture suddenly went, the screen filling with gray snow and the sound hissing with static.

"There," he said. "Got it."

Working quickly, he attached the connector to the back of the television. The hissing sound stopped and was replaced with silence. The screen cleared, but changed to blue, no picture.

"Didn't work," Travis concluded.

"Did too," a testy Nish countered.

"Where's your movie, then?"

"It's eight o'clock in the morning, Einstein. You think they put adult movies on at this time so little kids can watch them over their cereal?"

"There's nothing on at all," Travis said.

Nish smiled, confident: "There will be tonight."

After breakfast, the boys went outside, thinking they would head down to the lake and check out the old wooden toboggan run.

It was a fine morning, bright and crisp with the dew ice-cold and sparkling on the green-brown grass. A thick cloud seemed to have settled over the lake, and the boys, standing in sunlight with blue sky above them, felt as if they had entered another world. Travis shivered. He could almost see the head of a Brontosaurus rising through the cloud to stare at them.

"Hey!" Nish whispered, holding up a hand to halt everyone. "Look down there."

Down past the putting green and the tilted lawn chairs and the still-leafless hedge, three men were walking and talking quietly. It was the three coaches – Muck, Barry, and Ty – and all had track-suits on, though Muck's seemed more for comfort than workout. With his limp, he could never run. Barry and Ty were cooling down from a dawn run, both young men perspiring, both wearing head sweatbands, and Barry, the fitness nut, carrying hand weights he kept pumping as he walked and talked and listened to Muck. By the movement of the others' hands, the conversation was both animated and anxious.

The three coaches were coming up over the grass to the same side entrance the players had used the night before. The men had not yet seen the boys.

"In here!" Nish hissed.

Travis looked over. Nish was signaling to the other three boys from behind the garbage dumpster, which was just off to the side of the back entrance. It was a natural hiding space. But why hide? If Muck caught them, he'd kick their butts, for Muck always said he considered sneakiness a crime equal to stealing and lying, for in its own way it was both.

But the other boys were already squeezing in behind Nish. Travis hurried to join Data and Wilson in the gap, well out of sight but well within earshot. Travis caught his breath, nearly gagging.

"Smells like you slept here, Nish," Data hissed. "*He'So'!*" ("Stinks!")

The others giggled, including Nish, who then placed his index finger over his lips to shut everyone up. If they made a sound, they would be caught. If they were caught, they would be in trouble.

They could hear the three men coming, their low conversation rising with their steps until, finally, the boys could make out what Muck was saying.

". . . not the first time, and won't be the last. But I can hardly agree with such a wild idea as you're putting out, Ty."

Ty was talking low, his voice anxious to convince. "It's not the idea that's wild. It's Brown. He's a certifiable loonie. You catch him trying to bribe the kids, he gets a few drinks inside him and suddenly he wants revenge. And what's the best way to get at you? The team, obviously. The team collapses at a tournament like this, you end up taking the rap. Maybe you even lose the team next season."

"Makes no sense at all," protested Muck. He seemed upset with what he was being told.

"Muck, just hear Ty out," said Barry. "That's what I thought at first, too."

Ty continued: "I was doing the stats Tuesday when Brown came in with a new pair of braces he wanted to fit onto Matt's pants. He showed me the package. I just nodded and let him go on in and set it up. Who's to say what he did when he was in there?"

"But the point is," said a determined Muck, "why would he do it?"

"To screw you around. You lose your top forward, our best playmaker, you lose the tournament, you lose your position."

"That's me," argued Muck. "But why Sarah?"

"The best way to get at you," said Barry.

Ty laughed, exasperated. "You're missing a big point here, Muck."

"Which is?"

"Who told on him?"

Muck sniffed, considering. Thinking about Sarah coming to talk to him at Whiteface Mountain. He shook his head violently.

Among the eavesdroppers, only Travis knew what Muck would be thinking. Even if Mr. Brown hadn't actually seen Sarah telling Muck, he might have guessed. She was the one who'd walked away from him up on the mountain, after all. Mr. Brown would want to get back at her. And would want to get Muck, too.

Muck still wasn't convinced: "He wouldn't do something like that."

"He wouldn't, eh? What about last night?"

"He was drunk."

"And this morning he's sober. But he's still a loonie, drunk or sober."

Muck said nothing in response. The three coaches were at the door. Barry had it open for the other two, and in a moment the door clicked shut.

The four boys let their breath go and hurried

out from behind the dumpster to fill their lungs with fresh morning air.

"*He'So'!*" shouted Data in disgust.

"You hear all that?" asked Nish, his face alive with excitement.

"They think Matt's dad did it," said Wilson.

So, too, did Travis. But he also thought the Panthers had done it. And then he remembered why they had wanted to get up so early this morning.

"The camera!" he said.

The camera would prove who had been sabotaging them. The Panthers. Mr. Brown. Or no one.

"Let's get Norbert up!" Nish called.

# 14

The Screech Owls were not scheduled to play the Toronto Towers until 2:00 p.m. in the big rink, the Olympic rink, the rink where the U.S.A. had won the Olympic gold medal in 1980, the "Rink of Dreams" according to the postcards in the souvenir shops. That gave them the morning to get the camera out and examine the playback. They had to wait until Mr. Dillinger went up to the rink to unlock the room, and then they would have to figure out how to get the camera without him seeing.

It was simpler than they figured. The whole team knew of the camera, but only three would go up to the rink to get it. Norbert, of course, because he would be responsible in the end if they got caught or if the camera somehow got damaged. And Derek, because he had taken the keys and would also be in trouble, and because he had the most believable reason for being there, even if it was only to hit his father up for a few dollars for the arcade. And Travis should go, they decided, because he was the least suspicious of all the kids. If they sent Nish, alarms would go off in the mind of everyone who saw him. Nish, giggling, loved the idea that he was too dangerous to send.

The three boys, with Norbert carrying a shopping bag for the camera, got to the rink shortly after Mr. Dillinger had taken his keys and set off to begin preparing for the game. He was working a lot of hours for the team, sharpening skates, repairing equipment. Travis had never seen him so serious or caught up in his work. No jokes, no kidding, no pranks. He seemed to be taking the sabotage personally: as the one in charge of the equipment, he was probably blaming himself for letting it happen. But what could he have done, Travis wondered, stand guard twenty-four hours a day over the room?

Travis felt sorry for Mr. Dillinger. Here his son, Derek, was having the tournament of his life – almost entirely due to Sarah's problems – and he couldn't enjoy it. He had stopped whistling. He wasn't singing. Travis wished all this would just go away so they could have their old general manager and trainer back.

Mr. Dillinger was sharpening skates when the boys came along. The Screech Owls were, perhaps, the only peewee team in the world with their own skate-sharpening equipment, but Mr. Dillinger had suggested buying it and Muck had agreed and, after working more midnight bingos than the parents wished to remember, they had earned enough money to purchase a unit that could fold up into its own suitcase and be pulled out and set up in less than ten minutes.

Muck, who often said, "You're only as good

as your equipment," was delighted. Mr. Dillinger had worked with the entire team to find out who liked what and who played best with what kind of sharp. Dmitri, the quickest, liked his blades sharpened immediately before every game and ground so deep he could stop on a pin – a dime considered too much space for him. Nish, who liked to block shots, wanted a thin edge so he could slide more easily. Travis liked sharp skates, but not sharpened too deep, because he liked to work the corners and needed the flexibility. Muck figured the sharpening machine was worth a dozen goals a year to the Screech Owls. And a dozen goals a year, he said, could be the difference between first place and last playoff spot in the league.

"Hi, Mr. Dillinger," Travis said, as the boys came along.

"Hi, there, Trav –" Mr. Dillinger looked up. He nodded at the others. "Norbie. Son."

"You need any help, Dad?" Derek asked.

"Naw, not unless one of you wants to stand here for half an hour grinding Dmitri's skates down to his knees."

The boys all laughed. They were glad to hear Mr. Dillinger joking again.

"Anything happen?" Travis asked.

Mr. Dillinger smiled. "Just as I left it."

"Good."

"Let's hope that's the end of it."

"See any of the Panthers around?" Derek asked.

Mr. Dillinger considered for a moment. "I don't think so. I don't know whether I'd recognize them if I saw them. You still think they're the ones messing with Sarah's equipment?"

"Maybe."

Mr. Dillinger went back to his sharpening. "You might be right. You might be wrong. Maybe we'll never know . . . Travis, will you run in and grab your blades for me?"

"Sure." This was the opening they needed.

"And get Sareen's, too. Muck's thinking about starting her against the Towers."

"Got ya."

Travis and Norbert went into the dressing room while Derek stayed with his father, pretending to make conversation but really making sure Mr. Dillinger didn't follow the other two. It took Norbert less time to gather up the camera and equipment than it did for Travis to root his skates out of his bag and find Sareen's. They came out just as Mr. Dillinger was finishing up Dmitri's second skate, running a thumbnail along the edge to check it. He shook his thumb, wincing at the sharpness.

"Good. Thanks, Trav." Mr. Dillinger took Travis's skates and looked down at the bag Norbert was carrying at his side. "You been shopping, Norbie?"

The boys froze. If he asked to see what Norbert had bought, he would find out about the camera. If he found out what the boys had done – taken his keys, more or less broken in, set up a camera to spy – then heaven only knew what he would do about it. And what would Muck, with all his lectures about "sneakiness," have to say?

But Norbert was quick with an answer. "My mom made me buy some sweatpants."

"Good, good – okay, see you boys later. You be here forty-five minutes before we're on, okay?"

"Okay!"

"See you later, Dad."

"See you, Son."

They gathered in the health club off the pool area. No one ever seemed to be there working out, and no one was there this time, as they had been hoping. The entire team waited as Norbert flicked on the camera and checked through the screen to see if there was anything on the playback. Norbert stared, checked switches, checked the tracking count, then lowered the camera and looked up.

"We caught something."

"What?" Nish practically shouted.

"Don't know. Just know that something set off the activator. There's about thirty seconds of video run off."

The players' excitement rose and they pushed in closer.

"There's only one screen!" exclaimed Norbert. "I can't show everybody. Back off, okay?"

"Back off!" Travis repeated.

"We need a big-screen TV," said Nish. "Like they have in the sports bars."

"How would you know what they have in sports bars?" Wilson asked.

"I know."

"Biggest screen in the world was at the 1937 Paris Exposition," said Willie Granger out of nowhere. "Bigger than an Olympic ice surface."

"Just everybody back away," Sarah said impatiently. "Let Norbert check it and he'll tell us what we've got."

They backed off, waiting. Norbert raised the camera, the machine shaking from his nerves, and slowly he pressed the button to play the video.

"Hurry up!" shouted Nish. No one paid him any regard.

Norbert stared for what seemed like an eternity. The camera shook, the team waited.

"Someone came into the room!"

"Who?" Nish shouted for everyone.

"Can't see – only a back of someone moving across."

The team groaned as one.

"Wait, there's more!"

They waited, afraid to breathe. Finally, Norbert sighed deeply and lowered the camera. Norbert blinked several times, seemingly unable to speak. He looked like he'd seen a ghost.

"It's Mr. Dillinger."

"Damn!" Again, Nish spoke for all.

Travis felt his hopes sag. Of course, Mr. Dillinger must have been up to check last night. Travis had hoped the mystery would finally be solved so the tournament could continue without incident. He had hoped, in a way, that it would turn out to be someone they hadn't even thought of. Not Mr. Brown, because that would be hard on Matt, and not the Panthers, because that would be, well, that would just not be fair. No one played hockey that way, by hurting the other team's best player.

But all the ingenious activator had caught was Mr. Dillinger going about his business, unwittingly triggering the camera as he came in to make sure the Owls' equipment had all been aired out properly.

Travis walked up to the arena with Nish and Data and Wilson. They arrived more than an hour early, eager to get a feel for the game that was coming up against the Toronto Towers. They knew they had to win to make the finals, because they were tied with the Panthers at one win, one tie each, and the Panthers were scheduled to play the relatively weak Devils later, which should mean an easy win for the Portland team.

The Towers had a win and a loss and would have to win against the Screech Owls to make the final four. Another team, from Montreal, already had two wins and a loss, so there was no avoiding the importance of the Screech Owls' next match. If the Towers beat the Screech Owls, then Toronto might advance to the finals. The first-game tie with the Panthers was going to be of little help to the Screech Owls if today they added a loss.

When Travis walked in, he saw Muck walking toward him with a serious look on his face. His first thought was that there had been more trouble. But Muck wanted to speak to him about something else entirely, something completely unexpected.

"I've already called your parents, Travis," Muck said. "And they say the decision's yours. There's an area scout from the Bantam AA's here and he's asked for permission to speak to you and a couple of the other players. All I said was I'd present his case to the parents and player. And that's all I'm doing."

"What's it mean?" Travis asked.

"Maybe nothing. Maybe something. They can draw from a wider range than us and it's one of the best teams in the province – I know the coach pretty well, he's a good man – but it's tough to make and tough on parents. Both time and money. I think they play about 120 games a year if you count tournaments and exhibitions. But they're interested in you if you're interested in them."

"I don't know."

"You want to hear what he has to say?"

"I guess so."

"The arena manager's set aside a room for him. He's there now with the others. Just down past the washrooms, first door on the left."

Travis stared at his coach, trying to read Muck, but Muck was unreadable. It was impossible to say how he felt about this. It was almost as if it was none of his business, but it was all his business. He was the coach, after all, and Travis one of his players. Still, Travis couldn't play peewee forever. And if he ever wanted to make the NHL and see his sweater hanging up there with Terrible Ted's in Joe Louis Arena, then he'd have to leave Muck at some point. Perhaps this was it.

Muck turned to go, his expression giving away nothing. Travis didn't know whether Muck thought it a good idea or a bad idea. But that was Muck: he wouldn't say. It would be the player's decision. The player's and the parents'.

Travis headed back down the corridor. Mr. Dillinger was coming the other way, singing one of his stupid songs – something about a purple people-eater – and he gave Travis a shot in the shoulder as he passed. Mr. Dillinger knew.

Travis knocked at the closed door.

"Come in," a big voice called.

Travis pushed the door open. Inside, he saw the big voice belonged to a small man who was standing up and setting down a clipboard with writing on it. On chairs pulled around him were Dmitri Yakushev, Matt Brown, and Derek Dillinger. Maybe that was why Mr. Dillinger had been singing.

Dmitri was there for obvious reasons. Skill and speed. Matt Brown, Travis supposed, would have caught their attention through sheer size and his shot. And Derek, of course, was having the tournament of his life. Even if Sarah Cuthbertson had been able to play as she could, there might come a time when she wouldn't be here, as at some point she'd leave for a women's team.

"You're Travis Lindsay," the big voice boomed.

He seemed to be informing Travis rather than asking.

"Yes."

"I'm Pierre LeBrun. I'm with the Crusaders, Bantam double-A. You probably know Donny Williams, who was with Muck's gang two years ago."

"A bit."

"He's with us now. We like where he comes from. We like Muck's system. We like what we've seen here from you fellows this week. Have a seat, Travis."

Travis sat, and listened. Mr. LeBrun offered information, nothing more. The Screech Owls' players fell under the recruitment area of the Crusaders. The Crusaders were, as Muck had said, one of the best organizations around. Sweaters and socks and skates supplied. Some sticks supplied. Tournaments last year in Toronto, Lake Placid, Quebec City, and Vancouver. Tentative plans for a trip to Finland this coming winter.

*Finland.* Travis could hardly believe what he was hearing. Finland. Home of such legendary players such as Teemu Selanne and Jari Kurri.

International competition. He was already half-way to the Detroit Red Wings!

"I've already met briefly with your coaches," Mr. Lebrun told them. "And they have no problems with what I'm about to propose to you."

He waited a moment, smiling, the boys waiting.

"If you four are agreeable," Mr. LeBrun continued, "we'd like to send you invitations to attend our fall camp. I can't guarantee you you'll make the team, but from what I've seen here this week, I wouldn't want to bet that you won't."

Travis looked at the others, who were also looking around. None of them had ever heard such talk before. None of them knew what to say.

"Can I send you invites, then?" Mr. LeBrun asked.

"Sure," said Derek, his voice shaking.

"Okay," said Dmitri, his voice the same as always.

"Great," said Matt.

"Yeah," said Travis.

Yes, indeed.

# 15

"Sarah's sticks are missing!"

The voice was Ty Barrett's and it was coming from outside the dressing room, but everyone inside heard him. He was talking to Muck, who had just stepped outside to see how far the Zamboni had got with the ice cleaning. Muck swore – unusual for Muck, meaning he was very, very upset.

Sarah had heard as well. She had just finished tying her skates and pulling on her sweater and had her helmet, ready to strap on, in her lap, when Ty's voice burst in through the door. She didn't say a word, just shut her eyes and leaned back against the wall. Travis could hear her let her breath out slowly.

"Give us a break!" Nish shouted from behind his mask.

"How could they be 'missing'?" Jesse asked no one in particular.

The door opened and Muck came back in, his jaw working furiously but no sound coming out. He had no idea what to say himself. He signaled for Mr. Dillinger to come with him, and Mr. Dillinger, shaking his head and blowing air out of his mouth, hurried from the dressing room to consult. The players could hear more swearing, both Muck and Mr. Dillinger.

Muck returned again, followed by Mr. Dillinger, his face now red and angry-looking. "Someone's made off with Sarah's sticks," Muck said very matter-of-factly. "She'll have to borrow. Travis, you're a left. You have extras?"

"Two."

He turned to Sarah, her eyes now open, glistening slightly.

"You can try Travis's. If you don't like them, try some other lefts. We've got no choice."

Someone who doesn't play the game would never understand, Travis thought as the Screech Owls warmed up Sareen to start her first game of the tournament.

A hockey stick has a personality, Travis figured, and it gets the personality from the owner, the one who tapes it and bends it and handles it and feels it. Changing sticks in hockey is like a batter heading to the plate with a shovel in his hands, or a basketball player heading down the court in church shoes. It doesn't feel right, and when it doesn't feel right, it usually doesn't work right.

He had given two of his sticks over to Sarah and she had tried them but obviously was not content with them. Sarah liked to taper the top of her stick; Travis liked a big knob of tape. Sarah liked a fairly straight blade for playmaking; Travis liked as big a curve as he could get away with for roofing shots and corner-work. Sarah liked a short stick for in-close work; Travis liked one that stood to the bottom of his chin so he could get all his weight behind a slapper.

The only player who liked his sticks like Sarah was Dmitri, but Dmitri was a right shot. She tried one of Matt's sticks and one of Jesse's, but then came back to Travis's as the best of a poor choice. She seemed sadly discouraged during the warm-up.

The game went poorly. Sareen was so nervous she let in the first shot, a long dump-in from the other side of the blue line. And Sarah could not hang onto the puck at all. This time, however, Muck refused to juggle the lines to compensate. He seemed determined to go with Sarah at firstline center no matter what.

But the team was paying for her lack of stick control. With Dmitri at top speed heading in on right, she sent a pass that would normally have meant a breakaway but, thanks to the big curve, caught slightly and went behind Dmitri, throwing him offside.

And later, with Travis parked all alone at the

side of the net and Sarah with the puck in the slot, the Screech Owls lost the tying goal when Sarah backhanded the puck and it went looping off the other side of the curve into the corner and out of harm's way.

The Toronto Towers, knowing they must win to have any chance of going on in the tournament, fought ferociously and were up 2–0 at the break. The first goal had been Sareen's fault, the second had been Travis's fault. He had thought Nish had control of the puck and broke over the blue line toward center, only to have Nish checked off the puck. The Towers' defenseman pinched, picked up the puck, and hit a winger sitting on the far side of the net for a perfect one-timer. The goal light was flashing as Travis, feeling like a fool, was still on the other side of the blue line.

Finally, at the break, Muck had had enough. He put his arm around Sarah as he told her that Derek was yet again moving up onto the line and Sarah, fighting back tears, her lips trembling, had nodded that she agreed. Muck gave her a little hug as he let go.

The juggling worked again, just as it had for the first game. Sareen settled down and didn't let another goal past her. Derek played his heart out, scored once and set up Dmitri on a clean break away, which he cashed in. The score was tied 2–2.

Matt Brown scored the go-ahead goal on a Screech Owls power play, hammering a shot in from the point that seemed to tip in off a Toronto player's skate toe. And the Screech Owls' fourth goal was scored by Travis – but it was hardly one for the highlights.

With two minutes to go in a game the Towers had to win, they had pulled their goaltender, and Derek, stealing a puck inside his own blue line, had hit Dmitri for a second breakaway. But Dmitri, sometimes generous to a fault, had slowed down, drawn the one defender to him, and laid a perfect, soft pass to empty ice so it was sitting there, waiting, when Travis arrived at the front of the empty net. He could have scored with a bulldozer.

When they came off the ice after the handshake, Mr. LeBrun was standing to the side of the rubber

mat leading to the dressing room. He congratu-
lated each player as he or she passed, with a special
tap for the four with whom he had met, and a vic-
torious punch to the shoulder of a sheepish-looking
Derek Dillinger.

Mr. Dillinger, carrying the water bottles and
first-aid equipment a few steps behind, beamed as
he passed Mr. LeBrun and the scout said, "You got
a good one there." Mr. Dillinger knew; the whole
team knew. Mr. Dillinger was glowing red when he
came into the dressing room.

"All right, listen up!" Barry Yonson yelled
when the clatter of falling sticks had subsided and
everyone was in their seats and beginning to pull off
helmets and gloves. Muck wanted to speak to them.

"You can thank your lucky stars that was
Toronto and not the Panthers," Muck told them
in his usual quiet voice. "Most of you played like
house-league atoms out there."

The players knew it was true. Even considering what had happened to Sarah, the Screech Owls
had stunk. Had it not been for Derek's inspired
play when he was moved up to replace her, and

Sareen shutting the Towers out in the second period, they might have been packing up to go home.

"Pick up your sticks as you go," Muck said.

"Mr. Dillinger's going to lock them up in the van overnight. And Sarah, you go with Mr. Dillinger downtown. He'll take you to pick up some new ones, okay?"

Sarah smiled. She'd be able to play in the final. "Okay," she said.

"Alllll rightttt, Sarah!" Nish shouted.

"Yesss!" Derek added.

Good for Derek, Travis thought. He knows if Sarah comes back, he drops back. He knows who the real first-line center of the Screech Owls is. He knows what a team means.

# 16

The Screech Owls held another meeting in the unused health club. Travis was in charge. He was surprising himself the way he was starting to take command of things so easily. But since almost everything concerned Sarah, and Sarah was the captain, it seemed better that the assistant captain represent the team. And that was exactly what Travis was beginning to do.

"We almost blew it today," Travis said. Everyone agreed.

"Muck was right about what he said. Most of us – me included – played like atom house leaguers. We screw up tomorrow and we've lost the championship. We owe Muck better than that."

"It's hardly our fault," Data protested. "You have to consider what they've been doing to Sarah."

"That's right," agreed Gordie Griffith.

"We all know what's been happening," Travis countered. "What's happening to Sarah doesn't mean a thing on the scoreboard."

"It's true," agreed Sarah.

"Besides, Derek's been playing great hockey," said Travis. "We have to make sure we're all playing great tomorrow. So let's smarten up."

"What about Sarah?" Fahd asked.

"What about her?"

"What if they do something again?"

"The sticks are locked up in the van."

"What if they cut her straps?"

"I brought my stuff back," Sarah said. "It's safe in my room."

"You bring your skates, too?" Wilson asked. Sarah shook her head. "They're in with everyone else's in the big footlocker, under lock and key."

"What if somebody breaks into it?" Fahd asked.

"Who'd be able to tell my skates from anyone else's?" Sarah asked.

"Maybe it doesn't matter," Fahd said suddenly. "Who's to say they won't try something else now?"

Travis didn't follow: "Like what?"

"Like what if someone takes Derek's sticks this time?"

"They're all in the van."

"Or Dmitri's skates. Or slashes Guy's pads. If they can't get at Sarah, why wouldn't they get us some other way if they're already doing what they've been doing?"

As usual, Fahd's points were dead on. If the Panthers' purpose was to cripple the Screech Owls, and if stopping Sarah was no longer possible, then it stood to reason that they would have to be thinking of some other way. If Mr. Brown's purpose – and Travis still couldn't see that he had one – was to hurt Sarah, who had told on him, and Muck, who had humiliated him, then he would still want to get at Muck, and the only way left to him would be to go after Dmitri or Derek or Guy or Nish or, for that matter, Travis, who certainly wasn't going to have two bad games in a row.

Travis sighed, nodding. "Well, what do we do, then?"

"Bring all the equipment down to the hotel," Gordie Griffith suggested.

"Not enough room," Travis said.

"Van's already full of sticks," Nish added.

"Set up a real guard," Fahd said.

Travis didn't follow. Nor, from the expression on the faces of the others, did anyone else.

Fahd explained: "We tried the camera. It didn't work. Someone still got in. We need a real guard there."

"You mean a player?" Sarah asked.

"Yeah, someone who could stay in the room and make sure nothing happens."

"Sounds dangerous," Nish said.

Fahd considered a moment. "Maybe. But since the problem has always been equipment, all we'd need to do is know what they'd done. We'd have until four thirty to get it repaired. If we'd known about Sarah's sticks before the game, we would have had lots of time to get her new ones."

"That's true," said Nish.

"All we need is someone to watch and see if anything's going on. Then, in the morning, either we fix it or we get Mr. Dillinger to fix it."

"We should tell our parents," Data said.

"No way!" Nish argued. "You think they'd let us stay up all night in the arena?"

"Just one of us," said Fahd.

"One?" Nish asked.

"We also want to find out who it is, don't we?" Fahd asked. "We all go up there we're just going to scare people off. Besides, if we want to win tomorrow, the rest of us are going to need our sleep."

"Okay," Nish countered. "You got all the answers, Fahd. What're we going to do?"

"There're two lockers in each one of those rooms we're using to store the equipment, right?" Fahd asked.

Derek agreed. He would know. "One for sticks," he said. "One for whatever."

"We don't have our sticks there any more," Gordie said, as if settling the point Fahd was heading for.

"Exactly," Fahd said. "It's empty. It's got air holes. It would hold a player."

"Have to be awfully small, wouldn't he?" a sceptical Nish pointed out.

"Exactly," Fahd said.

He was staring directly at Travis.

"Too bad, sucker. You're going to miss the show!"

Nish was in his element: giggling, surrounded by wires, the back of the television in front of him. He was teasing Travis. They had to wait for Mr. Dillinger to come back from the rink so Derek could "borrow" the keys again and, in the meantime, several of the players had come up to Nish's room to see the promised spectacle: adult movies.

Nish had the protective coupler off again and was re-connecting the cable wires. Satisfied, he swung the television around and began playing with the channel switch.

There was a light knock at the door. The boys all jumped: *had the motel figured out what Nish was doing?*

"It's Sarah," a voice called. "And Sareen."

Nish began to glow like a goal light. Travis immediately jumped up to let the girls in. Some of the other boys began giggling.

"Come on, Nish," Wilson teased. "You promised."

"Promised what?" Sarah wanted to know.

"Nothing," Nish said, a bit too quickly.

"*Nothing?*" Wilson said with astonishment.

Sarah and Sareen looked at each other, then suspiciously at Nish.

"What's going on here?" Sareen asked.

"You keeping secrets from us, Nish?" Sarah added.

Nish gave up. "I'm trying to fix the TV so we can get free movies," he admitted.

"Come on, Nish, it's more than that," Wilson said.

Nish turned on him, scowling. "Thanks a lot."

Sarah giggled. "You're trying to see a dirty movie, aren't you, Nish?"

Nish was crimson now, shaking his head. "I just wanted to see if it works," he protested.

"And does it?" Sareen asked.

Nish turned, startled. "What?"

"Can you get them?" Sarah asked.

"I don't know."

"Well," Sareen said, "why don't you show us?"

Nish seemed completely baffled. "Not with you here!"

"Why not?" Sarah wanted to know.

"You're a girl!" Nish practically shouted, pointing out the obvious.

"Why, so I am!" Sarah exclaimed, faking shock. She looked at Sareen, pretending to jump back with surprise. "Why, look, you're one, too, Sareen!"

Sareen stared, surprised, at herself. "I am? I am! How does Nish manage to pick up these things?"

For once, Nish hated being centered out. "It's

not funny!" he protested.

"It is, too," Sarah scolded. "You want to watch men and women but you don't think it's right for women to watch, too. Isn't that it?"

"I just want to check. I don't really want to watch." This statement threw the rest of the room into howls of laughter.

"Put it on," Sareen told Nish. "We want to see, too."

"We're on the team, aren't we?" Sarah said, teasing Nish.

Nish seemed surprised. "You really want to watch?"

"'*Check*,'" Sarah corrected him.

Nish looked around the room for support. He was getting none. "Go ahead," Data said. "Everybody here but Nish already knows how we got here. He may as well finally find out." Everyone laughed. Nish shrugged his shoulders and went back to fiddling with the television, his color fading from bright red to pink.

He flew through the channels on the manual selector, some of the regular television channels coming in instantly, some of the pay movies as well. Data tried to get them to stick with a *Star Trek* rerun, but no one else was interested. A Western flicked on. And a thriller that some of the players recognized and wanted to watch again. But Nish was determined.

His hands fiddled and, suddenly, he came upon a channel with no picture, but sound. The sound was grunting.

"That's it!" shouted Data. "*Hljol!*" ("Beam me aboard!")

Everyone laughed, Nish included, delighted that the focus was shifting off of him.

"Bring in the picture," Sarah said.

"I'm trying, I'm trying," Nish said. His chubby hands flew as they worked on the horizontal and vertical hold. He had the adjustment box open and was working every possible dial, desperately trying to pull in the picture to go with the alarming sound.

An image caught and flew by, too quick to catch. "That's it!" shouted Wilson. "Go back!" Frantically, Nish fiddled the dial back. The picture flickered twice and then came into full, glorious color.

A wagon train was stuck in the mud. A team of mules was braying as they pulled, hopelessly. Two young cowboys were behind the wagon, up to their waists in mud, pushing and grunting. It was another Western.

"So that's how you make babies, Nish," teased Sarah. "Now you know the big secret."

Nish's color went back to goal-light red. There was another quick rap on the door. Nish punched off the set, panicking.

"Who is it?" Travis called.

"Me – Derek."

He had the keys. It was time to go. Travis could feel his heart stop dead, then start up again twice as fast.

# 17

Travis's heart was now pounding so hard he couldn't believe the rest couldn't hear it. Derek, with his dad's keys, and a few other Screech Owls – Nish, Sarah, Dmitri, Fahd, and Travis – had come up to the rink just before curfew and just as the last game of the evening was coming to an end. Unnoticed, they had slipped down into the dressing-room area and, with Dmitri on watch, were setting up Fahd's guard.

The empty locker easily held Travis. Closed, it

had enough air holes, probably for airing out figure skaters' outfits, that he could see out easily and even sit down and relax, the locker was so deep. But comfort was hardly Travis's first concern. He was petrified of what would happen when the lights went out! Petrified, and unable to tell anyone.

"I can fit here," Sarah said. "I should be the one staying. It's my stuff they've been after."

Fahd spoke for the others, Travis excepted. "You're our most valuable player," he said. "And you're still short of sleep from that first night."

Travis had wanted to beg her – anyone – to replace him, but didn't dare. No one knew about his dread of the dark, and now here he was about to be placed in a box – in a *coffin!* – and be buried alive in an arena dressing room.

"You try it, Nish," Travis suggested. "I bet even you can fit."

"No way," Nish said. "I'd get stuck in there and die."

Travis felt he was going to die himself. No one else was offering. Not Fahd, who was hardly as important to the team as Travis. Not Dmitri, whose scoring was possibly a bit more important. And certainly not Nish, who was also probably as important. He wished they'd asked little Guy Boucher to do it, or Sareen, who wasn't playing anyway but was desperate to do something, anything, to help her team.

But it was too late. Travis was assistant captain and he was expected to take responsibility. The others were completely caught up with enthusiasm for Fahd's idea and Travis had simply been carried along with them as they hurried to put the plan into action.

"You'll be all right?" Nish asked.

Travis had to lie: "Yeah."

"You're a braver man than me," said Nish. He had no idea, Travis thought.

"That's stupid talk," Fahd said. "You got some chocolate bars, an apple in this bag. There's a can over there if you need it, but you'd better use it before they shut down things or someone hanging around might get suspicious."

"What if they catch him?" Nish asked. Nish wasn't being in the least helpful.

Fahd was getting impatient with Nish raising the alarm. "No one's going to catch anyone," he said. "Travis stays put and doesn't move."

"What if they open up the locker?" Sarah asked.

Fahd had thought of this. "Travis can bolt it from the inside with this." He had a small pen-knife and showed them how it would lock in the latch so no one could move it from outside. "They'll think it's locked if they try it."

"You okay, then?" Sarah asked.

Travis looked up from the locker. She was looking at him like he was the greatest friend in the world. He felt as if he was doing something impor-tant, something vital.

"Fine," he lied.

Travis thought he was going to throw up. He had settled into the locker and they had closed the door and he had tried the knife bolt and tested it, and, satisfied, they had said their farewells to him from the other side of the air holes and left.

Derek wanted to get the key back into the hotel room in case his father noticed it was gone. He would sneak the key out again first thing in the morning, and they would, they promised, have him out of there by 7:30 a.m., in time for either the first serving of breakfast or a quick cat nap, whichever Travis felt he needed more.

When they left, Fahd turned out the lights.

*Total, unbelievable, suffocating, frightening, snake-filled dark!*

Travis felt himself begin to panic. His heart was thundering, his chest bouncing like a parade drum. He had his eyes wide open and it seemed he could see strange lights, reds and greens and flashes of orange, and then it seemed as if he could hear sounds, movement.

*Rats!*

No, it was nothing. Just his imagination. Water running through the pipes. The heat coming on. Doors slamming on other rooms as the rink closed down for the night.

Travis tried to think about the games he had played and the game they would play tomorrow against the Panthers. Slowly, gradually, his heart settled and the colors seemed to leave his eyes. Instead, as his pupils slowly adjusted, he began to make out shadows and forms beyond the air holes. There were still lights on in the corridor, and some of them were making it through the narrow little window in the door and around the corner of the entrance way. *He could see!*

Well, he could see a bit. But a bit was better than nothing. He figured in a coffin he would see nothing. And breathe nothing. This was bad, this was *terrible,* but it was not death.

He waited for what seemed like hours. To pass the time he began sorting through his hockey card collection in his mind, trying to think of ways to organize cards that weren't by year or whatever company had manufactured them. He put all his cards worth over twenty dollars – well, according to the book, anyway – together. He put all his Europeans together. All his Russians. He put all his good centers together and liked that.

Then all his good left-wingers, and imagined himself included.

He thought about all his autographed cards – Pavel Bure, Jaromir Jagr, Teemu Selanne, Paul Kariya, Adam Graves, Mike Modano, Gretzky – and he wondered how many times Gretzky had signed his name since the first kid asked for one. A hundred thousand? A million? He wondered how many hours, how many days, how many *months,* Gretzky had spent signing over his career.

He wondered if Wayne Gretzky had ever sat, as Travis Lindsay had sat, at the kitchen table endlessly practicing a signature. A printed *T*, a looping *L*, a huge, exaggerated *T*, an *L* that rolled off into his number "7" just as Gretzky would place that little "99" at the bottom of his name. He wondered if Wayne Gretzky's sister had ever teased him about practicing his autograph the way his sister had teased him, and he wondered if a few times Gretzky, like Travis himself, had wondered if there was any sense in practicing something no one wanted, at least for the moment . . .

He had fallen asleep. He was down on his

haunches, slumped, his head lolling and his hands between his knees. When he woke he did not know where he was, but then it came back, not as a memory, but as a sound.

*His heart pounding through his chest!*

There was a sound at the door. The scratch of a key being worked in and turned, first one way, then the other, and then the pop of air as the door opened. Beyond, in the pale light from whatever light was still burning, Travis could barely make out a hulking silhouette. Form but no identity.

The lights went on. Not welcome, but blinding. Even to Travis hidden in the locker. He moved closer to the lower air holes and blinked, waiting for his vision to return. The room seemed impossibly bright. His heart seemed impossibly afraid. He was shaking, sweating. He was terrified!

The hulk moved across the room, keys jangling as they went back into a pocket. The hulk moved, opened up the latches on the skate sharpening box.

It was Mr. Dillinger!

He had come to do skates. He had his keys out and was undoing the big footlocker that held the team's skates and was rooting around for those he needed to sharpen. Good old Mr. Dillinger. Travis wanted to burst from the locker and hug him, so glad was he to see that the invader was neither a Panther nor Mr. Brown nor some unknown murderer with a grizzled beard and tobacco spit running down his chin and a long sharp knife in his boot. But he knew he couldn't call out. Knew he couldn't explain.

He also knew there was now no danger of being found in the locker. Mr. Dillinger knew better than anyone that it was empty and why it was empty. He wouldn't look in.

Travis felt a fool sitting there watching Mr. Dillinger work. It seemed so, well, sneaky of Travis to be doing this. But he couldn't help but watch. And the more he watched, the funnier he felt.

What was Mr. Dillinger doing?

# 18

Mr. Dillinger had the skate sharpener open, and he had Sarah Cuthbertson's skates out. Travis could make out the little number "98" Sarah had painted in white on the heel – the number chosen to honor the year, 1998, when women's hockey became an official Olympic sport.

But Mr. Dillinger also had a hammer out, the hammer he sometimes had to use to straighten out a crooked blade. Travis couldn't remember Sarah complaining about her blades.

Travis was unable to see Mr. Dillinger's face. He could only see his hands, and what they were doing with Sarah's skates.

Mr. Dillinger set the skates in the skate holder normally used for sharpening, but the machine was neither set up nor plugged in. He took the hammer then, and very carefully, very slowly, worked it along the blade, hammering hard at times, and then pulling the skate off and eyeing it down the blade.

It seemed he was fixing something. Perhaps, Travis wondered, Mr. Dillinger had noticed something that Sarah hadn't mentioned. Or perhaps Muck had noticed something. Whatever, Mr. Dillinger worked over the skates for the better part of ten minutes before he made one final check of the blade line, seemed satisfied, and then put everything back in its place, including Sarah's skates.

He then locked everything back up again, checked the room one last time, never even coming near the locker, and then went to the door, where he turned out the light, plunging Travis back into his coffin panic, and eased silently out the door.

The key scratched quietly again, turned, and the door was once more locked solid.

It took another ten minutes or so for Travis's heart to settle and some of his sight to return. It seemed strange to him: Mr. Dillinger coming up here late at night – Travis checked his watch, the digital numbers glowing 12:45 – just to straighten out Sarah's blades. That was dedication.

Travis was wide awake when the kids returned to let him out. He had heard the rink attendants arrive before 7:00 a.m. and he knew then that his ordeal was over. He had survived the dark! He had been buried alive and was still alive! He felt prouder of himself than if he had scored a hat-trick in the final game. Well, maybe not quite that proud, but . . .

The key scratched again and Travis knew it would be Derek and the others. He was already out of the locker and waiting for them when they burst in, their faces so uncertain that he wondered if perhaps they were expecting to find a body hacked to pieces by a chainsaw instead of their friend who had just proved something important to himself, but couldn't tell anyone about it.

"You okay?" Sarah asked.

"Fine."

"No goblins," Nish giggled. Travis ignored him.

"Anything?" Fahd asked.

"I don't know," Travis said. "I'm not sure. Derek, you got a key on that ring for the skate box?"

Derek fiddled with the keys. "I guess so. Why?"

"I don't know. I just want to look at something."

Derek found the right key on the third try. The padlock came off, the lid up, and Travis, without explaining, reached in for the skates with number 98 painted on the heel.

"What're you doing with my skates?" Sarah demanded.

"Just checking."

Travis held the skates up to the light and turned first one, then the other, upside-down. With his eye, he traced the line of the blade and saw what he had been afraid he might see: the blades were badly curved. Deliberately bent by a hammer. Sarah wouldn't be able to skate the length of the ice on them. If she tried to turn, she'd either dig in and fall flat or slip away and crash into the boards.

"What's wrong?" Sarah asked.

Travis handed her one of the skates. The other he gave to Nish.

"They're crooked!" Sarah shouted.

"Somebody's bent them!" Nish added.

"Who would do something like that?" Derek asked.

Travis had no idea how he would tell him.

"I have to talk to you, Muck."

It would be wrong to suggest that Travis had never done anything so difficult before in his life. He had, barely an hour earlier.

Travis had only described what he had seen, with no suggestions, no accusations, nothing. But Derek had seen through it immediately. Derek had burst into tears in the equipment room and Sarah, also crying, had tried to comfort him, but Derek had shaken her off and, without another word, fled the room, slamming the door behind him as hard as he could pull it.

They had probably taken too much time to put the skates back and the locks on. When it came time to lock the door up again, they found they had no key – Derek had run off with it. And when they hurried outside to see if they could still catch him, he was nowhere to be seen. Nor was he back at the hotel. It seemed he had run away.

Travis had found the coach at the gift shop where Muck was buying a copy of *USA Today* and a pack of gum. Muck took him out into the sun room by the main entrance – no one there but a bellman dozing in the sun – carefully opened the gum and handed a stick to Travis and took one himself, slowly chewing as if the flavor mattered more than whatever Travis had to say to him.

"Okay," he said, "shoot. What is it?"

Travis found he could barely speak. Even with the sweet gum in his mouth, his throat was burning as if he were about to cry. But no tears came; nor, at times, would any sound. Muck waited patiently, saying nothing, slowly chewing and then snapping his own gum. Finally, Travis got it all out. The camera, the keys, the locker, what he had seen, the skates, Derek, the keys . . .

Muck took it all in without even blinking. When Travis had finished Muck sat, looking very tired, and stared for a long time at Travis, who figured he was about to get into trouble for the keys and for staying out all night.

Muck stared, shook his head, and smiled. "Hockey does strange things to people, Travis."

Travis had no idea what he meant.

# 19

With the championship game not scheduled until 4:30 that day, Muck and the coaches had time to meet first with Mr. Dillinger and then with the officials of the Lake Placid International. Some of the players who knew what was going on had told their parents, and those parents had told other parents, and so everyone pretty well knew what had happened. But no one knew what was going to happen next.

And they could not find Derek. Travis and

some of the other players had looked for him, and the keys, without any luck. Muck said he would find Derek later. He didn't seem worried about him.

Sarah and her parents set off early for nearby Plattsburgh, where there were two big malls and where they would have a larger selection of skates to choose from than the little Lake Placid sports stores could provide. Sarah seemed much relieved. Not only had the mystery been solved, but she was coming back to Lake Placid with a brand-new pair of pump CCM Tacks, and it wasn't even Christmas.

Muck posted a note on the bulletin board asking all the parents and all the players to meet in the Skyroom at one o'clock. There was no hint whatsoever of what he planned to do.

Travis sometimes got edgy before a big game, but he had never felt anything like this before. It seemed his heart was once again pounding through his chest. The parents were milling around talking in low, quick voices. Some seemed relieved, some shocked. Mr. Brown looked like he'd just won a game himself. It made no sense to Travis.

Muck came in and walked to the center of the room. He said not a word. The murmuring stopped. Every face – players, family, coaches – turned toward him, waiting.

"Everybody knows the story," Muck said. "I don't need to go over it all again. You know what happened by now as well as I do."

He paused. The audience shuffled, coughed, waited. No one dared to speak.

"This incident has left us in a strange situation. I am informed by the tournament organizers that any such interference with another team would have been cause for immediate disqualification and expulsion of the Screech Owls from the tournament. But the organizers say since it is our own affair involving only our own people, then it is up to us to decide how we will deal with the situation."

Muck paused again, letting those in the room consider his words. Travis was sure he could hear Mr. Brown muttering under his breath, but he couldn't make out what he was saying.

Guy Boucher's father spoke for everyone: "What is the status of our manager, Muck?"

Muck breathed deeply, thinking. "Our manager, Mr. Dillinger, has resigned his post this morning."

Travis could hear Mr. Brown muttering again. Something about "charges."

Muck quickly fixed Mr. Brown with the stare his players seldom saw and, once seen, never wished to see again. The stare of a laser beam burning through steel.

Muck was looking at Mr. Brown but speaking to everyone: "I have been around this coaching business long enough to know that sometimes we can all let a simple game matter a bit too much and, before we know it, we've made fools of ourselves without even realizing what we were doing. There are some fathers – and some mothers – in this very room who know what I'm talking about. Ripping the head off some thirteen-year-old referee. Swearing at some little kid just because he happened to run into yours. Yelling at your own kid after a game because he missed a pass."

"That's hardly the same thing –" protested Mr. Brown.

Muck's stare turned into a hard drive from the point, labeled. "I've even heard of grown-ups offering bribes to children," Muck said. "You don't get much lower than that in my book."

Mr. Brown looked down at his feet.

"Now," Muck paused. "Mr. Dillinger would like to say something to us."

Mr. Dillinger! He was coming into this room? Now?

The crowd murmured with dissatisfaction. No one wanted to see Mr. Dillinger again. Not after what he'd done. Some of them as long as they lived. Travis could see Mr. Boucher's jaw flinch. He could see Muck watching the parents' faces, not the door, which Ty Barrett was opening into the hallway.

It seemed every breath in the room was held. Not even Mr. Brown was muttering.

Mr. Dillinger came in, his head bowed, his usual bouncing walk gone. He walked slowly to the center of the room and stood beside Muck, his eyes fixing by turn on the floor and the far wall and on Muck, but not once on any of the players or the parents.

He took a long time to compose himself. He swallowed. He coughed. He seemed on the verge of tears. He seemed about to run. But gradually he was able to speak.

"I'm sorry," he said. He swallowed again, gathering himself. No one spoke. "I am the one who bent the skates. I hid the sticks. I cut the straps."

"Would you mind telling us why?" Mr. Boucher asked. There was anger, and disgust, in his voice.

Mr. Dillinger waited a long time before continuing. It seemed he could say no more. But everyone waited, demanding more.

Mr. Dillinger's voice choked: "I guess I did it because I didn't think I was hurting anyone."

He reacted to the sharp intake of breath that came from several in the room. Mr. Brown swore, a vicious word that Travis had never before heard any of the parents use. Muck's stare was like a slap in the face; Mr. Brown looked down at his shoes, shaking his head.

"You can believe me if you want or not believe me if you want," Mr. Dillinger said. "I'd never want to hurt Sarah. You have to believe that. I love that kid like she was my own."

"That makes precious little sense," said Mr. Boucher.

"I know," Mr. Dillinger stumbled. "I know that. But when the girls weren't able to play that first game and my boy got moved up to the top line, I had this crazy thought that maybe I could help him stay there and get noticed."

"At the expense of Sarah?" Mr. Boucher asked.

"No, not the way I was thinking. I figured she'd soon be leaving for another team. She'd be a top-level women's player no matter what. She was the only one whose career wouldn't be hurt by something like this."

"'Career'?" Mr. Boucher said with a snort.

"That's the way I was thinking. I was all mixed up. I just wanted Derek to have a chance to be noticed. If he played with Dmitri and Travis, he'd get his points. And that's pretty well what happened . . ."

Mr. Dillinger paused a long, long time. The room grew very uncomfortable. He coughed. He wiped his eye, missed a tear that grew and then broke, sliding down his cheek as he continued to talk to them.

"What I did was wrong. It was crazy. But I just wanted Derek to have this one chance –"

Mr. Dillinger began sobbing.

"I'm sorry," he repeated. He swallowed hard once more, turned, and left. Ty Barrett held the door open for him.

Mr. Dillinger paused at the doorway.

"Muck," he said. "I owe you an apology. I disgraced you as your manager."

Then he was gone.

The room was silent. Muck still stood at the center. He would wait for one of them to speak.

"What will happen to him?" Mr. Boucher asked. It was the question everyone wanted to know the answer to.

Muck shook his head. "I suppose that's up to us, isn't it? The tournament organizers want nothing to do with it. They say it's our affair."

"He should be kicked out of organized hockey altogether," Mr. Brown burst out.

"I suppose he would be if someone here wished to file a report with the association. I won't be. It will have to come from one or more of you."

"He betrayed a position of trust," Mr. Boucher said. He was so much calmer than Mr. Brown. And what he said made sense.

"He did," Muck said. "And I think he knows that better than any of us."

"Just so his damn kid could get ahead," Mr. Brown exploded.

Muck had had enough. "His 'kid,' Mr. Brown," Muck said with that voice that could wither a player at the far end of the bench, "is the one most betrayed here, would you not say?"

Mr. Brown, his face red as a tomato, could only shrug.

"What Mr. Dillinger did was wrong. Very wrong. He has admitted that and I, for one, respect him for doing so. But we have a saying on the Screech Owls: you're allowed one mistake."

"This is hardly the same thing as skipping a practice," Mr. Brown argued.

"I didn't say it was the same," Muck countered.

"But to tell you the truth, I'm less interested in what *we* think is right or wrong than what those who matter most here think – and they are Sarah Cuthbertson and Derek Dillinger."

"They're just kids," Mr. Brown sputtered, shaking his head.

"Exactly," Muck said, and turned and left the room, his two assistants falling in behind him.

# 20

Travis went out into the parking lot with the other kids. The parents went off down the hotel halls in smaller groups, buzzing with concern. Mr. Brown was talking too loudly, swearing. Mr. Boucher seemed to be the one they were listening to.

Travis couldn't figure out how he felt. He had liked Mr. Dillinger so much. In a crazy way he still liked Mr. Dillinger. He felt sorry for him. Sorry that Mr. Dillinger had wanted so badly for

Derek to shine that he had worked it so Derek would get a chance to shine. He felt sorriest for Derek.

"You're the hero!" Nish said, slapping Travis's back.

He didn't feel like a hero. He felt horrible. He felt as if he had ruined someone's life, for Mr. Dillinger's life was the team, the driving, the joking, the working. He was a good manager, darn it, and how could something like this ruin it?

"You can see how it happened, kind of," said Data. Data, always analyzing, always looking for explanations.

"How?" Nish laughed. "He shafted Sarah for his own kid's sake. Get a life, Data."

"He never would have done it if he hadn't known Sarah was going anyway," Data said. "It was kind of like he figured she'd understand."

"Yeah, right!" ridiculed Nish.

"Like she'd understand being kept awake all night, so long as it helped Derek," said Data.

"Derek's got nothing to do with this!" said Gordie Griffith sharply.

"Besides," added Data, "Mr. Dillinger had nothing to do with that first night. He said that was what gave him the idea."

"Who kept sending the pizzas then?" Nish asked.

"Maybe no one. Maybe it *was* a mistake."

"Mr. Dillinger admitted he'd made a mistake," Travis said.

"And that makes it all right?" Nish said with heavy sarcasm.

"No, it doesn't," said Travis. "But at least he had the guts to go in there and apologize."

"He had no choice," Nish argued. "Muck made him."

"I doubt it," Travis said. Muck would never force anyone to do anything.

Muck was coming out the door into the bright light, shading his eyes from the sun, searching. He was looking for the players. He saw the group talking and walked over.

"We have a center to find," he said when he got there. "Any ideas?"

He was looking straight at Travis. It seemed

that Travis had somehow become the team leader, the one who spoke for them all. But he had no idea what to say this time. "I don't know. Maybe down by the water."

Travis's hunch had been right. They had all started walking down the hill toward the lake, but Muck had stopped them in their tracks and sent every one of the kids back – except for Travis. He wanted Travis with him when they found Derek.

Derek was sitting on the end of the old wooden toboggan run by the park and the beach. He had climbed the fence and was sitting well out of sight, but Travis had seen a stone plunk into the water as he and Muck came walking down, and he knew immediately where it had come from and who had thrown it.

Muck seemed so casual about it all. He came and stood by the water, his hands in his pants pockets, looking out over the lake, giving not even the slightest hint that he knew Derek was sitting above him on the end of an ancient toboggan run.

"How're you doing?" Muck finally said.

Travis, who had come and stood beside his coach, knew Muck wasn't speaking to him. He said nothing himself, only waited.

Finally, Derek's voice broke. "Go away," he said. He was obviously crying.

Muck never turned to look. So Travis did not look. If Derek was crying it would be his business alone. They would not embarrass him.

"You'll want to get some lunch in you," Muck said. "You'll need energy for the game."

Derek bit off his words: "I'm not playing."

"We're on at four thirty," Muck said. "Your teammates will need you there."

Derek sniffed hard. "They won't want to see me."

"And why would that be?" Muck asked.

"After what happened," Derek snapped. As if he couldn't believe Muck's stupidity.

"And what was that?" Muck asked.

"Give me a break," Derek said angrily.

"You're not the one who needs the break, son."

No one spoke for some time. There was only

the sound of sniffing and the distant gurgle of a small stream heading into the lake.

Finally, Derek spoke again. "What's that supposed to mean?"

"Your father apologized to the team," Muck said. "And to the parents. And to the players."

"Big deal."

"It's neither a big deal nor a small deal with me, son. It's just a fact. I happen to think it took some courage to do that."

"He shouldn't have done what he did," Derek snapped, angry.

"That's exactly what he said, son."

"He had no right."

"He knows that. He said that, too."

Muck said nothing after that. Derek sat and sniffled, and a couple of times choked with new crying. Travis felt terrible being there, as if he was witness to something he had no right to see. He could only wait.

Finally, Muck broke the moment with a small, short laugh.

"What's so funny?" Derek demanded.

"Nothing," Muck said. "Just that I'm beginning to wonder if anything I say to you guys ever sinks in."

"I don't follow," Derek said. Neither did Travis.

"What is it I say to you more than anything else?"

"I don't know."

"Sure you do. What is it I say at every practice and before every game and between every period. One phrase. Always the same thing."

Derek said nothing. He was sniffing again. Travis knew.

"What is it, Travis?" Muck finally asked.

"'Hockey is a game of mistakes.'"

"You got it."

Muck said nothing more after that. He stood staring out over the water and, after a while, a sniffling, red-faced Derek Dillinger climbed over the fence and dropped down onto the sand beside them. He had said nothing either. Yet it seemed to Travis as if they had somehow talked it all out, that now they could get on with the game.

"Sarah'll need her new skates sharpened soon as she gets here," Muck said. "And I'm afraid we're missing the key to the skates box."

Derek sniffed once more, then sort of giggled. "I threw it in the lake."

Muck turned and stared at Derek. But it was not the stare he had used on Mr. Brown. It was the stare he used when a play had gone particularly well. "I'd have done it myself," Muck said.

Muck then sat down in the sand and removed his shoes and socks and rolled up his pants. They could see the scar on his bad leg, red and stretching practically from knee to ankle. It must have been a terrible break.

"How far out and how deep?" he asked.

"Not far," Derek said. "Over this way, toward the dock."

"Am I all alone?" Muck asked.

Immediately, Derek and Travis started taking off their socks and rolling up their pants to join in the search. Their track pants wouldn't hold in a roll, though, so they both yanked them off and tossed them up on the sand. They were in their underwear now, their skinny legs shaking in the cold.

Muck was already headed straight out in the water, his white, white legs growing pink, and then purple, as he calmly limped back and forth, looking.

The two boys followed, the water cold as the ice bucket Mr. Dillinger always kept handy at the back of the bench. *Who would keep it today?* Muck had them all join hands and they began working back and forth on a grid, the three of them shivering and shaking as they felt across the bottom with their toes for the missing keys.

"Anybody comes along and sees us," said Muck, "I don't know you two."

Shivering, their teeth chattering, Derek and Travis began laughing at the crazy situation they were in and Muck's silly idea that they could somehow all be strangers, two of them half-dressed, all holding hands as they waded back and forth in ice-cold water.

"Got 'em!" Derek shouted. He pulled the keys up on the end of his toes.

"Thank heavens!" snorted Muck. "I can't feel my legs any more."

"Me neither," said Derek.

Muck smiled at him: "And you're going to need yours today – mine don't matter."

# 21

Sarah was back with her new skates. The carton they had come in was under her stall, the wrapping paper all around her, the skates, tongues flapping, on her feet as she stared down at her new equipment, delighted.

The dressing room was busy, alive. It had all come down to this one game. Panthers versus Screech Owls. For the Lake Placid Peewee International Championship. For the chance to take a victory lap on the same Olympic ice surface

Team U.S.A. had skated on in 1980. For the tiny, gold-plated medals and Lake Placid tuques they were, rumor had it, going to be handing out to the victors.

And Sarah would be there to help them this time. There for the whole game, without anything to worry about for once. Travis felt wonderful inside, excited and happy and thrilled. The others were equally worked up. But Derek was dressing as if he was alone in the room, a hunched-over kid pretending to lose himself in the concerns of his hockey bag. Travis felt terrible for him, but happy that Derek was at least going to play. They would need him, too.

Muck came in and checked out Sarah's new skates. He whistled, impressed. "No allowance for ten years for you," he kidded.

"They'll need sharpening," Sarah said.

Muck strode to the center of the room. He stopped, staring about as he always did before his pep talk. But it was too early for that. He would always do the pep talk just before they skated out onto the ice, just as the Zamboni was finishing up the flood. Never at this point, when they were just arriving to dress.

He smiled quickly at Travis, then stared long at Derek, who did not look up. Muck counted heads, satisfied.

"We're all here now. So keep it down for a minute. I have something that has to be said to you."

The players all stopped what they were doing. Even Nish. This seemed unusual to them all, not just to Travis.

"I have been talking to the tournament organizers," Muck began. "This is, as you already know, an international competition. It falls under a joint agreement between the Canadian Amateur Hockey Association and U.S.A. Hockey. A number of restrictions apply."

Nish's mouth was as open as an empty net. What was Muck going on about? The other kids were all staring up, completely silent, waiting for him to make sense.

Muck watched Derek as he spoke. "One of those restrictions is that each team must have a qualified trainer with certified first-aid training at the bench. If you don't have the proper helmet you can't play. Don't have the proper neck guard, can't play. Same thing about the proper trainer. There's only one person affiliated with the Screech Owls who has all the training necessary and all the right certification. But only one person. It isn't me. And it isn't Barry or Ty."

The whole room could sense Derek lifting his eyes from his shin pads. It was almost as if he were just now entering the room, as if up until this moment he had been missing, as if someone had been in his stall but it was not the Derek Dillinger they knew.

"Mr. Dillinger?" Fahd asked.

Muck turned, nodding. "That's correct."

"But he's off the team!" Nish blurted out.

Almost as one, the team turned and stared, Nish glowing beet-red and wincing.

Muck stared at Nish, not at all upset. "Technically, you're not quite right, Nish. He resigned from the team. We always have the option open of refusing to accept his resignation."

Derek's eyes were closed. He was covering his ears, shaking his head.

Muck continued, loud enough so Derek had to hear. "It's a simple choice. No certified trainer, we can't start the game. And it's Mr. Dillinger or it's nobody. None of the other parents has it. And I, for one, happen to consider him one of the best I've ever worked with."

Derek caught at the mention of this. His hands came down. He stared at Muck, dumbfounded.

"He's the best skate sharpener I've ever had," Sarah said.

"Me, too," added Dmitri. Dmitri was beginning to panic that he wouldn't have his fresh sharp for the game.

Muck turned to Sarah. "You're the one who should say," Muck said. "You give me the word, and I'll see if I can find him."

Everyone turned to look at Sarah. She closed her eyes a moment. Travis could see her jaw working, her teeth grinding as she thought. She opened her eyes, swallowed, and began nodding.

"I think so," she said.

On the other side of the bench, Derek's head went down, shaking.

Travis and Nish could not resist. Wearing only their long underwear, their garters, athletic supporters, shin pads, and socks, they scurried along the corridor to the bench area and sneaked out to watch.

They could see Muck climbing up through the crowd, the parents surprised to see him. They gathered tight against the wall with him when he called them over with a quick wave of the hand. They could hear nothing, but they knew Muck was giving them the same story that he had just told the players.

Travis couldn't fight the thought: *Is it really true?* Was there such a rule? Did neither Muck nor Ty nor Barry have the right training? And if there was such a rule, how did the tournament committee find out that the Screech Owls were without a proper trainer? Or did Muck go to them instead of them coming to him?

There were a million questions in Travis's mind, none of them answerable, none of them even questions he wished to share with his teammates. It was almost as if he and Muck had a special understanding now, ever since the incident with Derek down by the water. And Muck had looked at him in a certain way before beginning his speech about Mr. Dillinger.

If Muck had fixed it so they had to invite Mr. Dillinger back, why? Because Muck figured he had learned his lesson? Or because Muck figured all the parents, including, and especially, Mr. Brown, had learned a lesson that couldn't be learned by a quick punch in a parking lot? Muck was a mysterious man to the players. They liked him, they *loved* him, but they didn't pretend to understand him.

And how would Travis himself feel about Mr. Dillinger coming back? He had thought the world of Derek's father before all this. But maybe this had all happened because Mr. Dillinger got mixed up. He got far too carried away with the thoughts most parents – just look at Mr. Brown – had all the time. Only Mr. Dillinger had a way to make them happen. It was wrong, but at least he had admitted it was wrong.

Travis figured he would let whatever happened happen. He could see the parents breaking up high in the stands. He could see Mr. Boucher pointing someone out to Muck. He could see Muck walking over to the other side, where Mr. Dillinger sat by himself, his elbows on his knees and his chin in the palm of one hand.

"He's going to get him," Nish said.

"Maybe he won't come," Travis said.

"He'll come," Nish said.

Nish was right. They watched Muck talk for a while and then they saw Muck reach down and take Mr. Dillinger by the arm and pull him to his feet.

Muck then turned and began walking away, back down to the dressing room. Mr. Dillinger, it seemed, had no choice but to follow.

Everything began to happen very fast after that. Mr. Dillinger came in, looking terribly sheepish, and immediately set about doing his work, just as he always did, except there was no whistling, no singing, no kidding around.

He took Sarah's skates and sharpened them as carefully as the Screech Owls had ever seen him sharpen before. He worked for a while, came back with them, had Sarah run a thumbnail over them, but he was still not satisfied with his work. He then took the skates back and sharpened them as carefully as if they were about to go on the feet of Wayne Gretzky himself. Then he brought them back, showed Sarah that he had even cut out and taped a small "98" on each heel, slipped them on her feet and tied them. When he looked up and Sarah quickly smiled a thank you, it seemed Mr. Dillinger was going to float away.

He put new tape on the equipment box and loaded the table up with three different flavors of gum. He filled the water bottles, set the warm-up pucks in Guy Boucher's trapper, and ran for a bucket of ice from the maintenance office. Mr. Dillinger was back.

But Derek wasn't. Not yet. He would neither look at his father nor acknowledge his presence.

Travis understood. It would take time, if even time could heal what had happened. It was, in a way, easier for Sarah to forgive than for Derek. Mr. Dillinger was his father.

Muck came in and stood in his usual spot as the Zamboni made its last circle. "You expect a speech?" he said when he had their attention. "I have nothing to say to you. You know who you are. You know how good you are. You know who you're playing. You know what you have to do. Now let's get out there and do it."

"Let's get 'em!" Nish shouted.

"One last thing," Muck said just as everyone was rushing to line up behind Guy. Everyone stopped in his and her tracks.

"Derek, you're going first line again," Muck said.

Derek turned, in shock.

"Take Travis's spot."

Travis never felt so happy to be demoted in his life.

# 22

The arena was filled to near capacity. Some of the other teams were waiting around for the awards ceremonies and most of the parents were still there as well. It was going to be the biggest crowd Travis had ever played in front of, and though he would have loved to have been lining up for the opening face-off, he was happy for Derek. Derek deserved it. Derek needed it.

They played both anthems before the opening face-off. First "O Canada," then, to a rising roar,

"The Star-Spangled Banner." The roar was just like the one in Chicago, whenever the Blackhawks played on television, only here the crowd and players were smaller. But just as excited.

Travis stood along the bench for the Canadian anthem, burning with his own pride, but it was nothing to what he could see in the brimming eyes of Mr. Dillinger, who was staring at Derek as if the boy himself were the flag.

What Mr. Dillinger had done was wrong, but Travis thought he now understood what Muck had been getting at when he said, as he had been saying for as long as the boys had been playing for him, that "hockey is a game of mistakes." The kids had always thought that meant poor decisions on the ice, but they now all knew it also meant bad decisions off the ice. Muck also said mistakes are things you can always fix. You stop leaving drop passes. You take that extra split second to look before passing. You don't just fire the puck blind from the point. And, Travis guessed, you stop trying to control things when you yourself aren't out there trying to play the game. And, most important, you never hurt your own teammate to do something for yourself. Once you start doing that, there is no team.

But now the team was back, and all together. Derek was back on the ice. And Mr. Dillinger was acting like Sarah's personal valet. Still, Travis couldn't help but watch Sarah carefully as she went into her first turn. The new skates glistened and sparkled, but they held. Perfectly. And when she began striding down the ice, she skated like the Sarah Cuthbertson who had been amazing them all since she took up the game and showed everyone that a girl can not only play, a girl can star, and, in the case of the Screech Owls, a girl can be captain.

Nish, of course, was as ready for this game as any in his life. He had swiped the official score sheet when Barry had it in the Screech Owls' dressing room to fill out, and he had figured out who the enemy was by name. The little blond defenseman was Jeremy Billings, the big dark center Stu Yantha. Nish liked to know names, and liked to use them, too.

He went after Yantha halfway through the

first period, with a face-off down in the Screech Owls' end and Travis on a line with Matt Brown and Gordie Griffith.

"Hey, Stu!" Nish called from in front of the net.

Yantha, waiting for the one linesman to bring a new puck for the other to drop, looked up, not knowing who had called his name.

Nish was grinning like he'd already scored. "I bet I know why your parents called you 'Stu' –"

Yantha just stared, baffled. Nish hit him hard and low: "'Cause they couldn't spell 'Stuuuu-pid!'"

Travis had never laughed through an entire shift before, but this time his sides were hurting when he came off. Yantha had chased Nish around the ice from the moment the puck dropped until Nish had raced off for a change. Yantha was so distracted he forgot all about the puck and had become consumed by his rage. If it hadn't been for the little defenseman, Billings, the Panthers would have been in real trouble.

Sarah was having trouble with her new skates. But it had nothing to do with sabotage. Twice during shift breaks she had loosened them and

Mr. Dillinger had massaged her insteps. She was cramping up in the stiff, new Tacks. But she was not quitting. She never missed a shift.

With a minute to go in the first, Sarah intercepted a Panther pass just inside her own blue line and, on a backhand flip that might have skidded away if she'd been using Travis's stick, she hit Dmitri on the fly. Dmitri raced in alone, deked the Panthers goaltender, and sent a backhand along the ice in through the five hole.

1–0, Screech Owls.

Mr. Dillinger almost went nuts. He jumped so hard the water bottles spilled off the back shelf and onto the floor. He whooped and cheered and, when Sarah came off, hit her immediately with a fresh towel and a full, salvaged water bottle. And Derek hadn't even been in on the play.

With Gordie Griffith struggling, Muck told Travis to take the next face-off, and the Panthers also changed, sending out Yantha's line.

"Nice shiner."

Travis wasn't sure where the voice had come from. Yantha was leaning down for the face-off, but suddenly he looked up and Travis could see the sneer of contempt through the shield.

"You're soon going to have one for the other eye, runt."

Travis said nothing. He won the face-off on a backswipe to Nish, but Yantha flattened Travis with a cross-check to the face before he could turn. The referee either didn't see it or didn't care, for there was no call.

Nish tried to hit Gordie Griffith with a cross-ice pass and shouldn't have. The little blond defenseman had read the play perfectly and zipped into the hole, gloved the puck down, and dropped it onto his own stick. With Nish already beaten, he was able to use Data as a screen and put one through Data's skates into the short side behind Guy Boucher.

Panthers 1, Screech Owls 1.

A tie game, with the buzzer going to end the first period.

At the break, Muck told them to watch their plays. "Don't take stupid chances," he said, without mentioning Nish's bad pass. He didn't have to say anything directly to the big defenseman. Nish looked like he'd just lost his home and family and television. He was pounding his fist on his leg, desperate for a chance to make it up.

Mr. Dillinger had Sarah's skates loosened all the way. He pulled them free and Travis could hear Sarah's sharp intake of breath as she realized her feet were bleeding. Both socks were pink with blood.

Mr. Dillinger seemed very worried. "Those blisters are breaking!" he said.

"Put some ice on them," Sarah said to him. Mr. Dillinger looked at Sarah, unsure, but the uncertainty vanished when he saw the determination in her eyes. He reached for the ice bucket, set it down, and began working handfuls of ice cubes over her feet. Sarah flinched from the pain but refused to give in, and when Mr. Dillinger pulled first one foot, then the other, down into the freezing bucket of ice and water, she actually seemed to sigh with relief.

If Sarah can do that, Travis thought, I had better do something with my good feet.

"You're better than they are," Muck said. "This game is yours if you want it."

Sarah's skating was becoming labored. She picked up a puck behind her own net but lost it trying to pivot out. The big dark center, Yantha, picked it up and flicked it fast, the puck hitting the back of Guy's shoulder and dropping just over the goal line. The Panthers' bench and fans let out a mighty cheer when the red light indicated what had happened. The Screech Owls' bench let out a collective groan. Travis flinched when he saw Sarah, completely out of character, smash her stick in half over the crossbar.

Panthers 2, Screech Owls 1.

Muck put Sarah's line right back out, and his hunch paid off. She won the face-off and hit Derek, on the left, who crossed the blue line and sent a long shot ricocheting around the boards to Dmitri, racing in on the right. Dmitri neatly deflected the puck back to Sarah, coming in late, and Sarah stepped past the defense, pulled the goaltender completely out of the net, and sent a back pass to Derek, who had only to tap it in for the tying goal.

The Screech Owls' bench went nuts. As pretty a set-up as they'd ever seen the magical Sarah create.

Screech Owls 2, Panthers 2.

Travis was sent back out at center, and again Yantha came on. This time the Panthers' big center butt-ended Travis right off the draw, sending him spilling down.

Travis found his footing just as Yantha came back for the puck from his defense. The big center had his head down as he picked a bad pass off his skate and did not lift it again until he reached the red line – by which time it was too late.

Travis hit him low and as hard as he could. He shut his eyes and drove as if he were going through a door, and Yantha crumpled over Travis's back, his feet flying out from under him and high up over Travis in a half-somersault where he landed hard on his back. The referee's whistle blew. He was pointing at Travis. His hand then indicated tripping.

Nish slammed his stick hard on the ice in protest. "No way! That was perfectly clean, ref!"

"Put a lid on it or you're off with him," the referee said to Nish.

The players were all milling around. Yantha was still down, moaning, so no one had to worry about him, but everyone else was looking for a partner to hang on to. The little blond defenseman, Billings, took Travis in his arms, the two of them struggling for show but uninterested in scuffling.

Billings was laughing. And he winked again. "Nice hit," he said, then released Travis.

The Screech Owls survived being a player short and, later in the final period, Yantha took a bad penalty when he went after Nish in the corner and the referee caught him for slashing.

"Stuuuuu-pid!" Nish called after Yantha as the big center angrily headed off to the penalty box.

"One more word and you're with him," the referee told Nish. Nish wisely shut up.

Muck put out a new power-play team: Sarah, Derek, Dmitri, Nish, and, on the point, Travis. Any other time he would have been left wing on the power play, but Muck wanted to keep his first line together and bring Travis up for the advantage, so point was where he put him.

Travis, unfortunately, had never before played the point. He had no idea what Muck was up to. All he wanted to do was make sure he didn't blow it and cause the winning goal for the Panthers.

Sarah controlled the puck beautifully off the face-off. She and Dmitri began playing what they called "Russian hockey" in practice, one circling endlessly back so it seemed like the whole team was going in reverse. They kept dropping the puck to each other as they circled, controlling, waiting until one of them saw an opening to shoot through.

The Panthers, bewildered at this seeming nonsense, put two players on Sarah, who was now carrying the puck in yet another circle, and Dmitri took the opening the moment he saw it.

Sarah hit him on the tape with her pass. Dmitri crossed the Panthers' blue line and stopped in a spray of snow, circling back again but staying onside, and hit Travis with a perfect cross-ice pass as Travis gained the blue line. Derek was on the opposite side, stick raised to shoot, and Travis dished off a quick backhand that Derek one-timed so hard it hit behind the upper inside bar and stuck, dislodging the Panthers' goalie's water bottle.

Screech Owls 3, Panthers 2.

# 23

There were only two minutes left. Sarah was buckled over in pain at the bench, the blisters all broken and the stiff new skates unforgiving. Muck didn't want to send her out again – didn't want to have to send her out.

He re-jigged his lines and put out his best checkers, Travis included. He told them to dump the puck when they got it and hold the line when they didn't have it. He was going for the 3–2 win.

The Panthers took out their goaltender. They sent out five forwards, including Yantha, and the little blond defenseman as the sixth player.

Travis had never in his life seen such effort. The little defenseman, Billings, led more than half a dozen rushes over those final two minutes. His last was an end-to-end race in which, with Travis almost hanging onto him, the little defenseman still managed to slip the puck through Nish's legs, danced to catch it, and rang a backhander off the crossbar and out of play before crashing into the boards with Travis.

The referee's whistle shrieked to call a break in the play. Travis could see that the referee did not have his hand raised for a penalty. He had been checking cleanly. He could hear the breathing of the little defenseman lying beside him, the little player's lungs seeming desperate for air.

Slowly they rose from the boards. The little defenseman looked at Travis, grinning, and Travis tapped him quickly on the shin pad. No one knew better than the two of them how close Billings had come to tying up the championship game.

There were only fifteen seconds to go. Muck signaled from the bench that he wanted Travis to take the face-off again, and Travis moved over and Gordie Griffith moved out. Travis could feel the fury rising from number 5, the big center, and when the puck dropped, Travis instinctively ducked, barely missing a vicious elbow.

Number 5 hadn't even considered the puck. His intention was solely to take out Travis, and then deal with the puck. But Travis, down low, was able to snake the puck out of the big center's skates. He rifled it off the boards back into his own end, where Nish was already back, circling.

All six Panthers rushed Nish in desperation, and he held the puck as long as he dared before looping a high backhander out that fell flat at center ice and died immediately. Gordie Griffith picked it up and he and Travis had a two-on-one, the little defenseman instantly back, with the net empty.

Gordie tried a quick pass to Travis, but the little defenseman again anticipated perfectly, the pass intended for Travis hitting him on the shin pad and instantly up to his stick where he charged again.

But it was too late. The buzzer went. Time had run out on the Panthers.

Final score: Screech Owls 3, Panthers 2.

Sarah Cuthbertson was first over the boards, barefoot. Her feet covered in Band-aids from Mr. Dillinger's first-aid kit – and Mr. Dillinger vainly trying to stop her from jumping – she came over the boards and hit the ice and slipped and skidded and fell and whooped all the way to Guy Boucher, who was already throwing his stick and gloves into the crowd.

The rest of the Screech Owls piled on, Muck grabbing Sarah around the waist and hoisting her high off the ice so none of the skates would cut her already injured feet. They piled on Guy, who had kept the goals out. They piled on Derek, who had scored the tying and winning goals. They piled on Travis, who had set up the winner. They piled on Dmitri, who had scored the first goal. They tried to pile on Muck and Sarah, but Muck kept turning and swinging Sarah so they couldn't get them, and so they piled instead on Nish because Nish was, well, Nish. And he deserved it.

Mr. Dillinger was on the ice now and he was hugging the players as if they'd just survived a plane crash. He was dancing, shouting, slapping, hugging. Travis saw him stop when he came to Derek and Derek, still deeply troubled, gave a weak smile and took his father's offered hand. A hug would have to come over time.

Muck was Muck. He carried Sarah back to the bench and set her down until the madness stopped, and he walked around shaking the hands of his assistants and players like he had to get going somewhere. It was as if he had expected this. And he had.

They lined up for "O Canada" and the awards ceremony. The tournament officials gave out gold and silver medals – just like in the Olympics – and the Screech Owls got to do their victory lap, Nish and

Gordie carrying the skateless, sore-footed Sarah, and then they lined up to shake hands with the Panthers.

Travis felt funny going through the line. These players had been regarded as the Screech Owls' mortal enemies all week, but he hardly felt any anger toward them. With their helmets off and their hair soaked with sweat and their faces so red with exertion, they no longer looked quite so big or quite so menacing. They looked like the Screech Owls. Not big, not old, but normal. And Travis wondered if perhaps, to some of them, he looked bigger than he was. He doubted it.

He came to Stu Yantha and the big dark center stuck out his hand as if they were meeting for the first time. Not the first time since he'd tried to remove Travis's teeth with a butt end, but the first time ever. Travis didn't even feel that Yantha knew who he was. Why would he? They shook hands and said nothing.

At the end of the line, he came to Billings, who was grinning with his hand out and another hand to put on Travis's arm. They paused and, for a moment, Travis felt as if he had won the Stanley Cup and the television cameras were watching him and Billings, like Crosby and Ovechkin, as they met at center ice. Billings knew exactly who Travis was and he knew Billings, and they had respect and admiration for each other.

"Nice game," said Billings.

"You, too," Travis said. It felt inadequate.

"Nice hit on Yantha, too."

Travis smiled, remembering.

Billings smiled back. "Clean, too."

Travis had never felt so wonderful. Mr. Dillinger had bought pop and chocolate bars for everyone. Muck had shaken each player's hand again in the dressing room. They had stared at and felt their medals – Nish said they were real gold – and tried on their Lake Placid tuques. Nish was wearing his pulled completely over his face, more like he was robbing a bank than taking off his hockey equipment.

And the Lake Placid tournament officials had come in and handed out trading cards, a pack for each player. Only they weren't the usual type of trading cards. No Gretzkys here, but Bouchers, Goupas, Nishikawas, Ulmars, Philpotts, Grangers, Kellys, Adelmans, Cuthbertsons, Yakushevs, Lindsays, Dillingers, Griffiths, Browns, Noorizadehs, Terzianos, and Highboys. That was why they had taken the players' photographs that first day. They were having trading cards printed up for each of them.

Travis spread his cards in his hand and stared at them. It was like he had opened a fresh pack of Topps and he himself had come spilling out in high gloss. There were two cards for his grandmothers. One for his parents. One for Nish, who insisted on a trade. And one for himself, forever.

Exhausted, delighted, he pulled off his skates and felt pain sear up through his leg. He looked down, baffled, and could see blood through his left sock. Not a lot, like Sarah had, but blood all the same.

He pulled off the sock, wondering. And then he saw it: his own blister, red and broken.

A blister – in old, broken-in skates?

There was only one answer: Travis Lindsay was growing out of them.

Limping slightly from the welcome blister, Travis left with Nish, the two of them examining the cards they had just traded with each other. Some of the others had already left for the hotel to check out for the long, happy ride home. Travis figured he would sleep – and dream – all the way. And the way things were going, perhaps he'd have outgrown all his clothes by the time he got back home.

"Lindsay!"

Travis turned, recognizing his name but not the voice.

It was Jeremy Billings, the Panthers' little defenseman – in Travis's opinion, the true star of this tournament. He waited. Billings walked up and pulled out his own cards.

"Neat, eh?"

"Yeah."

"You want to swap one?"

Travis looked up. Did he ever. But he had only one for himself, one forever.

He looked at his new friend, smiling, that same blond face in miniature on the card he was holding out face first. Travis looked at the card and realized, perhaps for the first time, the true value of a hockey card.

"You bet," he said.

"Sign it, too?" Billings asked.

Travis couldn't believe it. Someone was asking for his autograph!

"Yeah, sure. You got a pen?" Billings shook his head.

"I got one," Nish said.

Nish reached inside his jacket pocket and pulled out the pen from his "Stupid Stop" – the one with the disappearing bathing suit. Billings took it and signed his name on the card he was giving Travis. He paused halfway, turning the pen so he could see if what he had thought was right. Yes, the bathing suit was peeling off the bathing beauty.

He looked at Nish, who was beet-red and shrugging. No explanation required.

Billings handed the pen and his signed card over to Travis, who pocketed the card and then signed his own: Travis Lindsay.

Big, with an exaggerated *T*, a looping *L*.

And the number "7" tagged on at the end.

**CHECK OUT THE OTHER BOOKS
IN THE SCREECH OWLS SERIES!**

# FACE-OFF AT THE ALAMO

The Screech Owls are deep in the heart of Texas, in the southern city of San Antonio. The town is a surprising hotbed of American ice hockey, and the Owls are excited to come and play in the big San Antonio Peewee Invitational. Between games, they can explore the fascinating canals that twist and turn through the city's historic downtown.

The tournament has been set up to include guided tours of the Alamo, the world's most famous fort, where Davy Crockett fought and died. The championship-winning team will even get to spend a night in the historic fort.

The Screech Owls discover that the Alamo is America's greatest symbol of courage and freedom, and when Travis and his friends uncover a secret plot to destroy it, they must summon all the courage of the fort's original defenders.

# THE NIGHT THEY
# STOLE THE STANLEY CUP

Someone is out to steal the Stanley Cup – and only the
Screech Owls stand between the thieves and their prize!

Travis, Nish, and the rest of the Screech Owls have
come to Toronto for the biggest hockey tournament of
their lives – only to find themselves in the biggest *mess*
of their lives. First, Nish sprains his ankle falling down the
stairs at the CN Tower. Later, key members of the team get
caught shoplifting. And during a tour of the Hockey Hall
of Fame, Travis overhears two men plotting to snatch the
priceless Stanley Cup and hold it for ransom!

Can the Screech Owls do anything to save the most
revered trophy in the country? And can they rise to the
challenge on the ice and play their best hockey ever?

SCREECH OWLS

# THE GHOST OF THE STANLEY CUP

The Screech Owls have come to Ottawa to play in the Little Stanley Cup Peewee Tournament. This relaxed summer event honors Lord Stanley himself – the man who donated the Stanley Cup to hockey – and gives young players a chance to see the wonders of Canada's capital city, travel into the wilds of Algonquin Park, and even go river rafting.

Their manager, Mr. Dillinger, is also taking them to visit some of the region's famous ghosts: the ghost of a dead prime minister; the ghost of a man hanged for murder; the ghost of the famous painter Tom Thomson. At first the Owls think this is Mr. Dillinger's best idea ever, until Travis and his friends begin to suspect that one of these ghosts could be real.

Who is this phantom? Why has he come to haunt the Screech Owls? And what is his connection to the mysterious young stranger who offers to coach the team?

SCREECH OWLS

# SUDDEN DEATH IN NEW YORK CITY

Nish has done some crazy things – but nothing to match this! At midnight on New Year's Eve, he plans to "moon" the entire world.

The Screech Owls are in New York City for the Big Apple International Peewee Tournament. Not only will they play hockey in Madison Square Garden, home of the New York Rangers, but on New Year's Eve they'll be going to Times Square for the live broadcast of the countdown to midnight. It will be shown on a giant TV screen and beamed around the world by a satellite. Data and Fahd soon discover that, with just a laptop and video camera, they can interrupt the broadcast – and Nish will be able to pull off the most outrageous stunt ever.

Just hours before midnight, the Screech Owls learn that terrorists plan to disrupt the New Year's celebration. What will Nish do now? And what will happen at the biggest party in history?

# PERIL AT THE WORLD'S BIGGEST HOCKEY TOURNAMENT

The Screech Owls have convinced their coach, Muck, to let them play in the Bell Capital Cup in Ottawa, even though it means spending New Year's away from their families. It's a chance to skate on the same ice rink where Wayne Gretzky played his last game in Canada, and where NHLers like Daniel Alfredsson, Sidney Crosby, and Mario Lemieux have played.

During the tournament, political leaders from around the world are meeting in Ottawa. To pay tribute to the young hockey players, the prime minister has invited the leaders to watch the final game on New Year's Day. The Owls can barely contain their excitement!

Meanwhile, as Nish is nursing an injured knee off-ice, he may have finally found a way to get into the *Guinness World Records*. But what no one knows is that a diabolical terrorist also has plans to make it a memorable – and deadly – game.

SCREECH OWLS

**ROY MacGREGOR** was named a media inductee to the Hockey Hall of Fame in 2012, when he was given the Elmer Ferguson Award for excellence in hockey journalism. He has been involved in hockey all his life, from playing all-star hockey in Huntsville, Ontario, against the likes of Bobby Orr from nearby Parry Sound, to coaching, and he is still playing old-timers hockey in Ottawa, where he lives with his wife Ellen. They have four grown children.

Roy is the author of several classics in hockey literature. *Home Team: Fathers, Sons and Hockey* was shortlisted for the Governor General's Award for Literature. *Home Game* (written with Ken Dryden) was a bestseller, as were *Road Games: A Year in the Life of the NHL*, *The Seven A.M. Practice*, and his latest, *Wayne Gretzky's Ghost: And Other Tales from a Lifetime in Hockey*. He wrote *Mystery at Lake Placid*, the first book in the bestselling, internationally successful Screech Owls series in 1995. In 2005, Roy was named an Officer of the Order of Canada.